A Merchant's Tale

A Merchant's Tale

The Life of William Hay (1787 – 1858)

Margaret Rose

A Merchant's Tale
The Life of William Hay (1787 – 1858)

ISBN 1 898852 57 X

First published by The Shetland Times Ltd, 1999.

Cover illustration by Alexa Rutherford.

British Library Cataloguing-in-Publication Data
A catalogue record for this book is available from the British Library.

Printed and published by
The Shetland Times Ltd.,
Prince Alfred Street,
Lerwick, Shetland ZE1 0EP, UK.

To my cousins Jean and Don
who invited me to Shetland.

I should like especially to acknowledge James R. Nicolson for his book *Hay and Company*, which inspired the writing of this novel.

A MERCHANT'S TALE

Contents

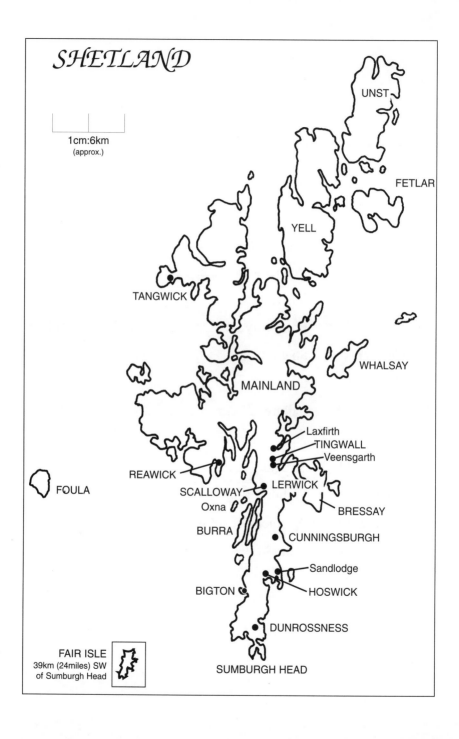

CHAPTER ONE

Childhood

"I won't take a shilling less," insisted James Hay, his brow furrowed with irritation and drumming his fingers on the table.

"There's a glut in the market," said his cousin Charles coolly, his dark eyes peering out of his rather ugly face. "It's been a good year, surely we can afford to bring the price down? Even then we shall still make a profit."

James scowled and paused.

He looked round the sparsely furnished counting house with its small high window and bare stone walls. The afternoon was wearing away and the sun shone obliquely into the room, leaving the corners in shadow. A couple of opened barrels stood against one wall and on the table were a ledger, a daybook, several quill pens, an inkstand and some sealing wax.

"Maybe you're right," he conceded.

Both men were in their late thirties, James, balding slightly with thin dark hair and a shiny, intelligent face, Charles Ogilvy with a shock of greying curly hair and a large nose. They were partners of long standing, used to seeking each other's advice, and knew they could trust one another.

"And what about the ship?" asked James.

"The weather's set fair for Norway and we've had a long run of good luck. The Revenue men don't suspect us, they've got their eyes on Malcolmson. Besides, there are too many of us for them to be able to pin anything on us. We've got a good skipper in James Clarkson. He's done the trip several times before. I think we can rely on him."

"That's all for now then," said James. "I must get back home."

"How's your wife?" asked Charles. "I suppose you're hoping for a son."

"Isn't that what most men want?" asked James. "I'm very fond of little Margaret, but I'd like a son."

"Don't let me hold you up," said Charles, standing up and buttoning up his jacket. "Let me know if there's any news. And I'll keep you in touch about all this."

James accompanied him to the door.

"You're right about the price," he said. "The market won't take it, I agree. Maybe a few casks of gin or schnapps..."

They smiled at each other knowingly. Charles waved his hand and walked off, leaving James looking thoughtful.

(2)

Several weeks later at James' house in Lerwick the nurse and a servant girl stood outside the half-open bedroom door whispering together.

"He seems to have quite lost his black moods and bad temper," said the girl.

"That's what having a son does for you," said the nurse. "I've never seen a more anxious husband. Last night he was in such a state and when he heard the news I think he was almost in tears."

"Can't make it out," said the girl. "He always seemed such a tough character."

"The baby's being called William after his grandfather," said the nurse.

"The old man who lives on Yell?"

"Yes."

Hearing James' voice calling, the nurse and servant pushed open the door into the bedroom. Through the window the morning sun shone in palely from a blue sky and they could see a wide stretch of deeper blue water and the light green outline of the treeless island of Bressay in the distance. Nearer at hand rose the masts of several sailing ships anchored in the harbour.

In the centre of the room in a large four-poster bed lay Mrs Hay, pale and smiling, a tiny infant in her arms. Next to her stood her husband looking proud and satisfied, his little daughter clinging to him as if the new intruder threatened to rob her of both her parents' attention. On a sudden impulse he gathered up his little girl in his arms and hugged her, bent to kiss his wife gently on the cheek, then straightened himself and moved quickly to the window. At once he caught sight of a ship busy furling its sails.

"The mail boat's come," he said, like someone suddenly waking out of a dream.

"I must go down for news."

The nurse rapidly made way as he passed them with a smile on his lips and an almost jaunty step.

(3)

William Hay was born in the tiny town of Lerwick in Shetland in the spring of 1787, two years before revolution broke out in France and six years before the war began. No ringing of bells saluted his coming, not even the firing of the cannon from Fort Charlotte, which overlooked the harbour. But for James it marked a special stage in his life.

At the age of sixteen, James had been sent down south by his father to Perth to study the linen trade, because some of the lairds on the island of Yell had been persuaded to try and introduce the industry into Shetland. Two years later James returned home and became manager of the linen factory at Catfirth, but after a few years it had failed, mainly because the lairds had wanted all the profits for themselves and there was little benefit for the workers.

James' father had been a tacksman, managing estates for profit, which in Shetland involved not only dealing in agricultural produce such as potatoes, but in salted fish. Nearly every Shetlander lived within reach of the sea, and part of the tenure of their crofts depended on fishing for their lairds. So that when the linen factory failed it seemed natural for James to follow in his father's footsteps and become a trader, importing the timber from Norway that was so vital in a land where there were no trees, as well as dealing in fish. Since Viking times when the Norsemen had invaded Shetland and given their names to every part of the landscape, ships had called there from Norway. In later years Hanseatic merchants from Bremen and Lubeck had come to trade in fish, and after the shoals of herring had deserted the Baltic and moved to the North Sea, large numbers of Dutchmen had come each year for the herring fishery. Of more recent years were the whaling boats from Hull and Aberdeen, who called at Lerwick to complete their crews on their way to Greenland, and there were the trading ships bringing up goods from Liverpool or Dundee. It was because Lerwick was very much in touch with the world's doings that James had moved there, building himself a warehouse with an outlet into Bressay Sound, where boats could tie up and unload directly. He also owned a store that sold all the everyday things that people needed, as well as stocking items required by seamen setting out for Greenland.

Local people eagerly awaited the arrival of the mailboat from Leith as it not only brought up stores but also the latest information from Edinburgh. It was news from Hull, where James had relations with two of the whaling companies, that he was expecting at this moment. As he left the house and made his way along Lerwick's only flagged street, so narrow in some places that two carts could scarcely have passed one another, he had an overwhelming desire to stop and tell someone he had a son. He hardly saw the prosperous two and three-storey houses standing incongruously at angles to one another along the street, or noticed the seamen lounging outside the liquor stores looking the worse for drink although it was still early in the morning. Nor was he conscious of the pervading smell of tainted fish in the air, something he always recognised when he arrived back from journeys south.

3

He hurried on down to the warehouse, passed out onto the quay, and quickly pushed out the rowing boat tied up there. Like all Shetlanders James was adept at handling a boat, in spite of the stiff breeze and slight swell. Other skiffs were pulling out for the mail boat, and among the huddle of people waiting on its deck he caught sight of a merchant he knew from Aberdeen. He redoubled his efforts. Spray splashed onto his balding head, spattered his breeches and dark coat with tails. When he had seized the rope ladder and clambered aboard, and shaken his colleague's hand warmly, the merchant exclaimed smiling, "Delighted to see you Mr Hay. I see you are well. I hope you have good news for me."

Unexpectedly forgetting the cares of business, James smiled broadly and said emphatically, "I have indeed good news. Yesterday my wife gave birth to a son."

(4)

When William was four and his brother Andrew two, a third son, James' namesake, was born. His mother never fully recovered from the birth, and died soon afterwards. This painful experience, tinged with an aching sense of loss, of loneliness and longing, was one of his earliest memories. For years he nursed a hidden feeling of hostility towards his new brother who seemed to have taken his mother away. He remembered his Aunt Grace, his father's sister, coming to take charge of the house and care for the tiny baby and three sullen children.

One day William came into the room where his father was sitting, to find him weeping uncontrollably. James, who had always been moody and subject to fits of anger, had sunk into a deep depression from which for weeks no one could rouse him. For William the belief that you could always rely on an adult to be in control had been shattered. He had felt close to his father, and now he felt doubly orphaned. Running to Aunt Grace he clasped her knees and buried his face in her lap, sobbing, "Why is Father crying? And where is my mother? I want my mother."

Just then the baby began to howl in its cradle, and Aunt Grace had put William down and gone to the door and pleaded with her brother, "James, they are her children and if you loved her you must care for them."

And James had made an effort, and tried to assuage his grief by listening to William's earnest prattle.

But from then on, it needed only a frustration, a disappointment, or a loss to bring back James' feelings of blank despair, and William and his brothers and sister grew up in the shadow of his black and sometimes violent swings of mood.

As the children grew older, their father's material affairs prospered. James bought boats for fishing and to transport timber from Norway or salt from Liverpool himself. William's Uncle Ian was captain of one such boat. He was a big gruff man of few words, who used to call in between trips to bring James news and report on his voyages. William liked him. He remembered the deep anxiety that hung over all the family when he was small, when Uncle Ian failed to return to harbour for two days during a storm. Instead of getting on with his lessons, he stood with his forehead pressed against the window, watching the raindrops bounce off the flagstones outside, the puddles whipped up into little whirlpools by the ferocious wind, and listening to the rain pounding on the roof, a constant reminder that something awful was happening. Then there was the infinite relief and rejoicing when the news came that Uncle Ian had sailed into Lerwick harbour safe and well, having been blown off course to the east for two whole days. His uncle suddenly became someone very special in William's eyes, because of the dangers he had been in.

The sea dominated William's young life. One day James took him with him to visit a family of orphans who lived in a croft down the coast. It was the first time William had visited such a humble home. James had to bend his head to pass under the low doorway into the dwelling, and once inside it was difficult to see at first for the smoke from the peat fire seemed to have no exit. A careworn thin-faced woman, a baby in her arms, and two toddlers clinging to her skirt got up as they arrived. Two other untidy youngsters stared at William suspiciously. The earthen floor smelt damp and the fire did not give off much heat. A table and benches, a wooden sofa, a rush basket or two seemed to be the only furnishing, except for two heavy dark wooden cupboard beds at the far end of the room.

"The bairn's been crying all night and I haven't had any sleep," began the woman, and then as James placed a basket of goods on the table. "I don't know how to thank you," she said.

"I promised your husband," said James simply. "He was a good man."

On the way home William asked his father about the family.

"The father was drowned during the haaf fishing last summer," said James. "A sudden storm. When that happens, the family is destitute unless they've got relations who can help them. Willie saved my life once and it's the least I can do to try and help his family."

On the other hand, on summer nights, seemingly endless, the sea could be calm and blue, and then it was a pleasure to learn to row and sail, and pit their wits against the waves and the wind. Nothing could compare with the joy of messing about in a boat, with birds flying overhead, the sound of the oars in the rowlocks, the gentle splashing as they hit the water, or the flapping of the sails against the mast. William learnt competence and independence and understood that to take risks could be fatal.

At the same time he felt a keen sense of rivalry with his brothers, particularly with Andrew, who always seemed to do everything better than he did. Only two years younger than William, Andrew was practical and intelligent, strong and healthy and bubbling with enthusiasm for life. Compared to him William was the dreamer, sensitive, creative and therefore more vulnerable.

One sunny evening, when the two boys had been taken out in a small boat learning to sail, across the sheltered waters of a small bay down the coast, and Andrew had seemed to excel at everything they did, William was suddenly conscious of an intense resentment against his brother, and feelings of jealousy. "Why is Andrew always better than I am? Why does he always get praise?"

William wasn't able to analyse his emotions, or to reason that if Andrew was the more competent, William was single-minded and would win through in the end. But those carefree days were marred by such negative feelings, and he did not always enjoy them to the full.

Outdoor summer activities were a balance to the strict classical teaching they were receiving from a local schoolmaster, for James had determined to give his sons a better education that he himself had received. All their sporting endeavours gave William a sense of freedom that he would later recognise as something very precious in life.

(6)

William's father was respected as a successful merchant and had become the largest buyer of fish in Shetland. Merchant buyers from London, Liverpool, Glasgow and Edinburgh would place their orders in January or February and James would travel south to do business with them. He would also spend several months reaching agreements with the local lairds and fish curers about supplies of fish to be sent to him. In September and October the fish was collected in barrels from the haaf stations round the islands. After October the sea was too rough and consignments were delayed until spring.

James also acted as agent for whaling companies in Hull and Aberdeen, whose ships sailed regularly to Lerwick to complete their crews. The shipowners would write to him early in the year, saying which ships would be coming up to Shetland that season and how many men they would require. James would set about recruiting the men, either among those who had sailed before, or from men who requested to be taken on. From early March onwards the tall-masted whaling-ships appeared in Bressay Sound and signed up their crews. They stayed long enough to take on equipment and stock up on provisions. James supplied them with goods like tea, coffee, sugar and oatmeal from his store, and was responsible for paying the men a month's wages in advance and instalments to their families. After four or five months when the ships returned, the crews celebrated in Lerwick by spending their money and getting drunk, often starting fights with local men. Most of the Shetlanders preferred to invest their earnings and buy a part share in a fishing boat. James made frequent trips to Hull to arrange matters with the whaling merchants and was in regular correspondence with several of them.

With the wealth he earned James invested in property and land in Lerwick.

From an early age William grasped that his father was also engaged in smuggling.

One day he was with his father at the warehouse when a stranger arrived by boat with several sealed casks. He was a tall flaxen-haired Norwegian and he sat drinking with James in the warehouse and talking in broken English.

Suddenly he pointed to William.

"Does the boy know?" he asked.

"About the goods?" asked James.

The man nodded.

James looked at William.

"William, do you know what is in these casks that Mr Svenson has brought over from Kristiansund?"

William shook his head. He realised that this was a serious moment, that he was about to be let into a secret of the adult world.

"It's spirits," said James. "Gin and brandy. It's come from Norway. Now, it's very important that no one should know that Mr Svenson has been here, and no one must ever know about these goods. Do you understand? If you were to let anyone know, they might come and take me away. Now will you promise not to say anything to anybody?"

William solemnly promised. Later he learned that contraband goods brought over from Norway or Rotterdam were concealed in a hidden passageway leading from the warehouse. He noticed that whenever his father had visitors and offered them a drink there was always an air of secrecy, and similarly with the tobacco they smoked. James also went off on odd assignments for a day or two up the coast to Laxfirth or down to Cunningsburgh and returned at night with a new cargo.

When the Dutch herring boats, known as busses, with their shiny oak sides and gay flags, congregated in Lerwick harbour in June, Dutch skippers would invite James on board. William once accompanied his father in a rowing boat to where several boats were moored so close together that you could climb a plank from one to the next. They had clambered aboard and down a companion ladder into a cabin that stank of stale herrings, to find a fair, tousled-headed Dutchman almost incoherent with drink. His eyes were glazed and he gesticulated alarmingly. William remembered being afraid and clinging to his father. But as the man didn't appear harmful, they were able to back out and climb onto the next bus. Here in a tidier boat an affable Dutch skipper with piercing blue eyes had offered James a glass of schnapps, and had spoken in Dutch which James seemed to understand quite well. Afterwards they had come away with a gift of spirits concealed in a cask intended for salted herrings.

Nearly all the merchants of Lerwick and district and many of the lairds too were engaged in smuggling. The authorities tried hard to stamp it out, confiscate goods and prosecute those concerned. But James, like other Shetlanders, thought it was worth taking the risk and breaking a law he felt was unfair.

(7)

William soon learnt that trading was a somewhat hazardous occupation. If the summer weather was stormy, or if catches were few, then the trade in fish was poor. If too many boats reached market with salted fish at the same time, then prices would be low. James was constantly in contact with family and friends to seek out new markets. When William was small he had even travelled as far south as the Mediterranean to try to establish links with buyers of fish in Barcelona and Marseilles. William recollected that he had come back talking of grapes and apricots and oranges, of dark-eyed and vivacious people, of wide waterfronts with fine merchant houses and exchanges. Very little profit had arisen from these trips and in spite of all his travels he seemed to be very pleased to be home in his own northern treeless land, where mists would drive in from the sea and where only social gatherings relieved the darkness and monotony of the long winters.

There were times when in spite of all his efforts trade was bad. Then James would grow moody and silent and sit hunched up for hours with frustration and sadness, overcome by depression. To disturb him risked a sudden outburst.

Almost unconsciously William gradually realised that the atmosphere in which he lived was a constant battling with fate, sometimes riding high, sometimes in the depths of despair, being ready to risk everything in the hope of profit.

When released from their studies, William and his brothers would be taken on Shetland ponies the six miles through the hills to Scalloway harbour, the sturdy little animals picking their way through the trackless bogs and ravines. What road there was was little more than a quagmire, and when they reached the top of the hill above the old capital of Shetland, they would pause for breath, to look down and point out the Scottish castle, now in ruins, silhouetted against the sea.

"Wicked Earl Patrick's castle," they would exclaim, and remember tales they had been told of how the Stewart lairds had oppressed the Shetland poor.

Or they would be rowed down the coast in an open boat and across Mousa Sound to the island of Mousa with its Pictish broch, where they could watch the seals or the sheep, picnic on the beach or climb up inside the mysterious old tower with its thick walls and steep steps.

For a boy growing up, far from the cramped and dirty towns of the south, it was a healthy environment. While many of the countryfolk in Shetland lived in poverty, tied to their crofts and their fishing and in bondage to their laird, William's father already had a position in local society which commanded respect and offered him certain privileges.

(8)

There was always a great deal of coming and going in James Hay's house. Merchants and cousins, friends and other visitors exchanged greetings and learnt of each other's doings. While revolution wracked France and destruction and the desolation of war followed throughout Europe, during William's childhood in Shetland there was no fighting. In Lerwick there was a garrison stationed at Fort Charlotte and soldiers were often to be seen in the street, the red coats of the officers creating a splash of colour amidst the grey surroundings. Several of them visited James quite frequently, sometimes took tea with Aunt Grace and enlivened the boys' lives with talk about distant places, about people and events in Scotland and England.

So too did naval officers from brigs and cutters moored in the harbour. For James such contacts were more than mere entertainment. Besides enjoying their society, he gleaned useful information from his visitors about trade routes disrupted by the war, kept in touch with former business acquaintances in countries hit by the British blockade of shipping and sometimes learned of friends whose business had been destroyed. Often James was invited on board to dine with the officers.

There was one young officer, tall and handsome with a dark moustache, whom William secretly admired. He plied him with questions about his ship and his life at sea, till his father, for once in a good humour, had begged him to excuse his son. The young man often seemed to be in Lerwick and William sought out his company whenever he arrived at the house.

Then suddenly he disappeared and to the boy's disappointment didn't come back again. Another officer who knew him explained that he had been sent home.

"Why did they send him home?" asked William.

The officer smiled and hesitated.

"He fell in love with a local girl. But his family doesn't want him to marry her. So they sent him away."

William considered this for a moment and persisted.

"Why don't they want him to marry her?"

At this point their conversation was interrupted and the officer's attention was drawn elsewhere.

William reflected that the adult world was full of contradictions he couldn't begin to understand. He returned to fancying himself in naval uniform and going to sea as an officer.

(9)

However, when he was about ten, an event occurred which changed his way of thinking.

One day he and Andrew had been out riding and had gone down into Lerwick intending to go to the warehouse where James was overseeing the arrival of a cargo of timber. It was a spring morning after a shower and the houses were shining damp. The street was narrow, and in front of their father's store a group of youths were lounging and talking.

Suddenly a number of officers appeared in the street from the direction of the Custom House and rushed towards them. The youths ran for it and dispersed in several directions, speeding up the narrow alleyways. One youth fled down the street towards William and Andrew but an officer was too quick for him and arrested him before their eyes.

"It's the pressgang," whispered Andrew to William.

Suddenly out of a store came a pale thin woman and her equally pale but beautiful daughter and began pleading with the officer.

"Don't take my son away," she said in her soft accent. "They'll capture him and put him in prison in France and I'll never see him again. And who will feed my family? My husband was drowned two years ago."

10

The officer had seized the young man by both arms and pinned them to his sides. He stopped and looked hard at the woman. She had begun to weep, her large blue eyes filling with tears.

"Please let him go," pleaded the girl. "Else we'll starve."

The officer hesitated. He was tall, dark and good-looking with the pink cheeks of youth. He was embarrassed and obviously not enjoying doing his duty. And the girl was beautiful.

"Go, I didn't see you," he said hastily to the boy, pushing him towards his mother. The other officers had disappeared in pursuit of their prey.

"Go," he said urgently.

In a moment he too had disappeared.

"Why do you think he let him go?" Andrew asked his brother as they moved on.

William was puzzled too and shaken.

"I don't know," he said. "That was Angus Malcolmson. Don't tell Father."

(10)

As a child William had an experience that recurred often in dreams and woke him up bathed in sweat and trembling. He had been taken on a journey by two of his father's friends by pony up into the hills. He wasn't sure where they were going. It was a grey afternoon and quite light as they travelled up and down the valleys over brown peat moors and yellow tussocks of grass, here and there passing a silent stretch of water. There was not a soul about. They reached the top of a hill expecting to command a magnificent view but instead saw heavy white clouds rolling in from the sea, a dense enveloping blanket of mist that came so fast it quickly shut out the landscape and took away their sense of direction. Huddled on their ponies they decided to turn back, as there was no well-defined track and they still had some way to go. So they turned and set off but within minutes reined in their mounts and came to a halt, declaring they had not passed that outcrop of rocks on their way before. Several times in the drizzle they stopped and set off again in a different direction, scaring groups of sheep looming out of the mist, until at last they admitted they were totally lost. William felt a sense of panic rise in his chest because he had always thought he could rely on grown-ups and because he was terrified they might become separated and lose him as well.

The winter afternoon was drawing in and if they didn't get back soon it would be dark. Finally one of the men suggested they let the reins drop and see if the ponies could find their own way. Sure enough, skirting ravines, jumping little rivulets and feeling their way through the boggy ground, the riders clinging for all they were worth to shaggy manes, the ponies managed to bring them safely down into the valley. Soon they came upon the scarred cuttings in the hillside where the local people had cut their peats, and they knew they weren't far from habitation. That was how William learnt to trust the Shetland ponies, and soon forgot the relief he felt when he got back, soaked to the skin, and could sit round a blazing peat fire and drink hot tea.

He heard his father express his concern for his safety and relief that they were back.

"He's a plucky young boy," said one of the men. "He didn't seem afraid. I thought we were lost for good."

But William had been afraid, and that fear he had experienced as they were swallowed up by the swirling mist returned to haunt his dreams.

(11)

It was when William was about ten that he saw his first whale kill. He had accompanied his father down the east coast of Mainland to the laird's mansion at Sandlodge where he had gone to discuss business. The mansion stood near the sea at the end of a pretty bay flanked on either side by low hills. Compared to his own home in Lerwick the home of the Bruces was imposing, and William was a little in awe of the laird with his tall stern figure and bushy grey eyebrows. But it wasn't his host that he remembered best of that long day.

As they were preparing to leave four fishermen arrived in a boat at the little beach and rushed ashore with the news that a company of whales was approaching a little way down the coast towards Hoswick. This was of great interest to James, for he sold blubber and whale oil, and if there were whales to be killed and he were on the spot it would be a fine opportunity to do a deal.

So they said their goodbyes and hastily skirted the coast southwards, as fast as the rough terrain and their ponies would allow. When they reached Hoswick they found the narrow shelving beach full of people of all ages, boys, women and fishermen, gathered together from all the nearby crofts. Everyone was in a high state of excitement. While the women in their wide skirts and plaid shawls scoured the beach for the larger sized pebbles that lay about on all sides, the men were feverishly stowing home-made harpoons away and launching their boats. Some were filling the bottoms of their boats with the pebbles, to frighten the whales.

William had heard many tales of whaling, of the dangers involved in getting close enough to the whale in a small rowing boat to be able to throw a harpoon, the risk of the animal diving and taking the rowing boat with it, or rearing up and lashing with its tail so that the boat would capsize. He had heard tales of heroism and disaster, but up till now he had never seen a whale kill.

He gazed eagerly out to sea with a mixture of curiosity and apprehension. At first he could only see the heaving of the sea in the distance, each wave edged with a little splash of foam. Then from time to time he would see cascades of spray high in the air as the whales rose to the surface to blow. He caught glimpses of huge sleek dark bodies rising into the air with the fluke disappearing last into the water. After they had dived there was a pause and then they would reappear somewhere else. It was obvious there was a large number of them.

Already a large fleet of fishing boats had collected from up and down the coast gradually approaching beyond the whales in a wide semi-circle. James explained the strategy to William. A few of the boats would stay outside the cordon to be ready to intercept any whales that might try to change course.

Fortunately it was a clear breezy day and the sea not too rough, a pale sun picking out the waves as they rose and fell. It needed a great deal of skill to row against the swell and keep the boats steady. James and William stood looking for a long time, straining their eyes as the local fishermen joined the others in a wide sweep round the whales. Several times the animals would disappear and appeared to break out, but by rowing for all they were worth the men managed to contain them and force them to keep moving towards the shore. They did it by shouting at the tops of their voices and by flinging pebbles into the water.

At length as the afternoon wore away the whales drew very close, obviously terrified of their pursuers, and began to roll about in the shallows, creating an uproar. The huddles of women and boys on the beach began to shout. The animals lashed wildly with their tails and William could see how huge and powerful they were. They aroused his admiration and for a moment he thought what a terrible thing it was to kill such magnificent beasts.

Then the killing began. Two men waded deep into the cold water, raising a harpoon above their heads, lifted up a fin of the nearest whale and forced it to roll over in the water. William, though weary, stood tense with excitement as they dug their harpoons hard towards the heart. The whale immediately went into terrible convulsions, lashing out with its tail in all directions and threatening to kill the men or drown them in spray. Then it lay still. After a pause it shuddered from time to time. Then the whale lay dead on the beach and as blood poured into the water William closed his eyes, but only for a moment. Fascinated, he watched as with loud cries other men attacked the nearest whales, sparing not even females and their young. He noticed that boys not much older than he was were joining in the killing.

Soon the little beach was strewn with dead and dying whales, and the edge of the sea had turned a bright red. A great stench filled the air.

James told William that now the men would begin to separate the blubber from the meat, and would probably come back and work all through the summer night. Each whale would yield a barrel of oil, and today's doings would ensure a full larder for the fishermens' families for some months to come.

As William mounted his pony and prepared to leave, strange emotions stirred inside him, feelings he was almost afraid to recognise. For one part of him was proud to have shared in this massacre, almost relishing the violence of the killing, as if by being present and accepting it all without flinching, he himself had been accepted into the world of men.

He found it difficult to forget that scene of carnage and as they rode off he looked back. It seemed as if the whole sea ran with blood.

(12)

Two of the most substantial houses that William visited regularly as a boy belonged to Charles and Thomas Ogilvy, who were James' cousins. Like William's father they were both successful merchants and Charles, as a young man, had worked with James and shared in some of his more daring smuggling ventures. He had a warm personality and had married a pretty, sweet-tempered wife with flaxen hair and blue eyes, who had given him, by the time that William was ten, seven children, six girls and a boy, the eldest girl only a year younger than William.

William felt at home in their house; their way of life was somewhat similar to his own and the same sort of people visited: officers, and naval officers, the magistrate, visiting merchants and other visitors to Shetland. William enjoyed playing with his cousins when they met, as they did frequently, on family occasions such as birthdays and christenings, at Christmas and Easter, and he and Margaret and their brothers appreciated the kindness of their Aunt Barbara, who paid them extra attention because they had lost their own mother. There was also a special warmth and security that did not exist in his own home, where they always had to be careful of their father's dark moods. When he grew up and looked back on his childhood, William realised that even if he had been denied something vital to life in the loss of his mother, he had learned what love and happiness were from his Uncle Ogilvy's family.

Uncle Thomas had the same pronounced jaw and very intelligent eyes as his brother Charles. He had a gruff sense of humour that William did not always understand, but he liked him because his uncle talked to him as an equal and made him feel grown up. Aunt Andrina, however, was a proud, rather reserved woman who seemed to have little affection to give her own four children, all of them under five, and none to spare for their cousins. She seemed relieved when the nurse took them away and she could talk to James.

14

Aunt Andrina's house was comfortable with thick carpets on the floors, and in the drawing room an elegant fireplace with gleaming polished brass. But it was not a place where the children felt free to play; to be themselves. They were expected to be on their best behaviour or earn a reprimand. They preferred going to Charles Ogilvy's even if their sister teased them for wanting to play with girls.

Charles Ogilvy's youngest was a fair, pretty child called Joanna. She was just beginning to learn to talk and was the delight of all the family. Even William and Andrew conceded that the little girl had charm, and Margaret enjoyed playing with her rather than with Uncle Thomas' daunting children.

So William was devastated to learn, first that Joanna had gone down with a fever, next that she was dangerously ill, and then that she had died.

It was a blustery autumn day, the sky dark and squalls of rain beating down from time to time when the family, except the very youngest, gathered to follow the tiny coffin to the kirk. William had been too young when his mother had died to take in what had happened: now he absorbed every detail. As the minister took the service in the bare cheerless church up on the hill overlooking the town, a great solemnness overtook the whole family, and he recognised the sense of grief as something he had already experienced in his young life.

Afterwards as they saw the coffin being lowered into the ground, and the clods of damp earth being thrown upon it, he knew instinctively that Uncle Charles' house would never be quite the same again, for them or for him. He supposed that this was one of those things that Uncle Thomas had tried to talk to him about, death at sea, women, drunkards, poor people and other areas of life as yet beyond his understanding. He watched the relations stand round the grave, lining up to share their condolences, watched his pale, tight-lipped father bend to kiss Aunt Barbara on the cheek, squeezing her hand and unable to say a word, and he felt tears come into his own eyes. But he fought them back, aware that it wouldn't do for his girl cousins to see him weep. At that very moment he began to grow up, and, like an ancient sailor leaving the safety of the coast and venturing into unknown waters, he was moving beyond the easy assumptions and securities of childhood into the mysterious, exciting and sometimes frightening world of adolescence.

CHAPTER TWO

Education

William spent the greater part of his youth in Aberdeen, where he and his sister went to school, followed later by his brothers. Although he had always known that he would go south to study, it came as a shock when the date for leaving Shetland approached and he would have to face a new life in Scotland on his own. Not entirely alone, because it had been arranged that Margaret should attend a boarding school for girls nearby, and there would be the opportunity to see each other from time to time.

He would always remember the seemingly endless journey south by sailing ship, buffeted by stormy winds and high seas, the cramped conditions below, the seasickness, with always the fear that they might be captured by French privateers or even sink before they reached port. There wasn't much to do on board except, when weather permitted, walk to and fro on deck watching the constant movement of the sea, and the white foam as the ship ploughed its way through the waves, listen to the squeaking of the masts and the flapping of the sails overhead, with the taste of salt on their lips. William wondered all the time what the future held. What would it be like to mix with boys from a big place like Aberdeen, perhaps more worldly wise than he was? Would he make friends and be able to hold his own? How he would miss his beloved Shetland! Fortunately like most young people he couldn't imagine very far ahead, and there was his sister to think about, suffering from seasickness and much more fearful of how things would turn out.

It was early in the morning with the sea somewhat abated and a pale sun trying to shine through the clouds that they came down the low coast of Scotland and sailed up the Dee estuary to the port of Aberdeen. There was general relief on board that the long ordeal was over and they would soon be approaching dry land. Already the Kirk of St Nicholas could be seen rising above the town, and William's mood changed to excitement and curiosity. There was something very appealing about arriving by sea, and he could make out the landscape as the low coast gradually edged nearer, the outline of grey buildings, and when they got close other ships in the harbour, a revenue cutter, dark-sailed fishing boats and coasting vessels, some setting sail and ready to leave on the high tide. Next he caught sight of sailors manning the yards, fishermen on the quayside mending nets, men busy loading a boat from carts, with the horses patiently waiting. He heard the seagulls crying, and the shouts of men working. Once they had gone ashore and felt the reassuring solidness of motionless earth beneath their feet, he found himself in the midst of a colourful bustle of people in front of a long row of unequally tall wooden buildings.

James knew Aberdeen well. He had arrived there in all weathers, and could handle the clamouring porters. He sent one to fetch their trunks, and asked to be taken directly to the home of Mr Macdonald, a merchant acquaintance with whom William was to lodge. During the week he was to attend the Grammar School.

As the pony trotted along and they bumped up the cobbled streets, William stared at the tall-storied houses built of grey granite, with dark slate roofs, which looked rather forbidding even in the sunshine as they drove up into an elegant square with a huge market cross and the Tolbooth with its steeple. Then they went on to a street in the north of the town called Gallowgate where the Macdonalds lived. Margaret, her dark ringlets reaching down onto the shoulder of her mantle, and her teeth clenched tightly together, huddled closely to her father. William, in spite of the long journey, looked eager and his eyes were shining. James' face expressed the pride he felt on bringing his two eldest children to study in Aberdeen.

Mr Macdonald was tall, very slim and dark, rather solemn with little to say to the children. But when Mrs Macdonald appeared, she proved to be short, round and lively, and anxious to look after them. She took them to see where William was to sleep and saw to the stacking of his trunk in the corner by the little window. The truckle bed had a gay quilted counterpane and on the wall hung a sampler someone had worked of the 23rd Psalm.

When Mr Macdonald called from below they went downstairs. He and James had plenty of news to exchange. They drank tea, lit their pipes and chatted, making plans for him to visit some of his other acquaintances before he left. James always seemed more animated in company than at home.

Then the moment that Margaret had been dreading arrived. James took her with her trunk of belongings off to the boarding school where she would live.

William suddenly felt his heart sink, when he realised that he was now alone, for the first time in his life. Alone to make his own mistakes, with unknown people and in unknown surroundings.

(2)

After two days visiting suppliers and customers, James caught the mail-boat home, which left in the evening because of the tide. William soon began to settle down and tried to concentrate on his new life. The Macdonald's were a strict but loving couple who had no children of their own but would like to have done so. Mr Macdonald had a small warehouse at the back of his house and a counting house where he and a clerk organised the business. Life was not so very different from home. The rhythms of life and the concerns of every day were already familiar to William. He missed his younger brothers, but here he felt grown-up and independent.

The time soon came when Mr Macdonald took him down to Schoolhill and introduced him to the headmaster of the Grammar School. It was a chilly September morning with more than a hint of autumn in the air though the sun shone brightly. William's new starched collar rubbed his neck and he felt self-conscious in his new dark school suit. On reaching the low grey building they went in under the belfry into the central courtyard, past the main assembly hall and straight to the Headmaster's study. There a dark man of medium height with dark eyes invited them in. He shook hands with Mr Macdonald and offered him a seat. William stood with his hands clasped nervously behind his back.

"This is William Hay," began Mr Macdonald. "He'll be living with me during his schooling. His father is Mr James Hay of Lerwick. I believe he has written to you."

The head slowly turned his gaze on William who returned it steadily.

"I have had the privilege of meeting Mr Hay," he replied. "Here we teach the classics, Latin and some Greek. I understand you have done some classical study in Shetland?" And he proceeded to ask William some searching questions to try to discover what the boy knew.

"Hmm," he said non-committally.

"I had thought perhaps Robert Gordon's Academy," murmured Mr Macdonald. "But his father insists he come to the Grammar School. I suppose he will become a merchant."

"You cannot beat a good classical education," said the head, gesturing with his hands in the manner of a teacher. "Not everything is useful but the classics lift the mind to higher things."

"I'm afraid I did not have that opportunity," said Mr Macdonald.

"Classics and good discipline," continued the head, handling the cane which lay across his desk, as William looked on in dismay. "Boys can be very wild."

The sight of the cane and the head's last statement did not do much to reassure the boy. So many ideas were running through his head. Was he to grow up to be a merchant like his father? Apart from a brief dream of becoming a naval officer, he had not yet really given the matter much thought. Up till now he had grown up in a merchant's world where every new relationship was put to good account. New acquaintances were valued as prospective buyers, or suppliers, or simply as useful sources of information. Profitability was the standard by which every aspect of life was judged. Perhaps there were other worlds he had not dreamed of where different values reigned and where his own personal abilities could be recognised and grow.

The head and Mr Macdonald had bent their heads low together and were conferring over matters such as fees and holidays. William stared out of the window into the courtyard where boys were now pouring forth in twos and threes to huddle in groups and play noisy games. A hum of boys' voices reached the head's study. He rose and opened the window, calling someone by name. A tall slim dark boy appeared at the door, addressing the head in terms of respect.

"This is William Hay," said the head, putting his arm on William's shoulder and pushing him forward. "He's to study with you. See you make him welcome."

With hardly a moment to say goodbye to Mr Macdonald, to whom he already looked for support in spite of their short acquaintance, William was suddenly propelled into the hurly-burly of the recreation period, like being thrown to the wolves.

(3)

William gradually settled into his new life as the autumn winds blew, mild at first and then cold from the east, and the leaves fell off the trees and were whipped up by the wind into little dances along the cobbled pathways. The first frosts began to bite, and some days thick Scottish mists came in from the sea and covered the town with a damp clammy mantle that obliterated all distant views. He was lonely at first. In spite of being of an out-going nature it took time to get used to the school routine, prove himself and earn a place with the others. So many things were unfamiliar and everything seemed bigger and more important than in Lerwick. It took time to make friends, to know whom you could trust and who would let you down, and William at first was glad to get back to the Macdonalds' to the warmth and comfort of a hot meal and a warm fire, where Mrs Macdonald took an interest in his doings, and gave him encouragement when he needed it. For him she grew to be the mother he had lost, while for her he represented the child she had never had. This was a blessing for a boy far away from home, though like all youngsters he tended to take his good luck for granted.

At the Grammar School the boys came from a variety of backgrounds. Some of them had fathers who were tradesmen or small merchants, but there were others who practised law or medicine and some of the aldermen of the town. William found his studies quite difficult at first. Many of the boys had a better grounding. Much of the time they spent construing Latin grammar, or painstakingly translating classical authors. There were four classrooms opening off the inner courtyard, and he was in the lowest, but he had a doggedness and a determination not to be beaten and did not stay long at the bottom of the class.

As the winter came on the classrooms were draughty and bitterly cold, in spite of the wood fire that stood in the corner of each room. It often sputtered with smoke and then it became hard to concentrate and William's mind wandered easily.

During the recreation period he often tried to stay behind near the warmth of the fire. Soon after his arrival some of the other boys started to tease him, because he was new and because of his different accent. Then they took to shunning his company altogether, going off in little huddles and leaving him alone. One morning, Donald, the boy to whom he had been introduced on the first day, found him huddled up indoors with his hands in his pockets, looking miserable, pretending to keep warm but really taking refuge from the unkindness of his schoolfellows.

"Aren't you coming outside?" asked Donald. "It's not as cold as all that." Then quickly summing up the situation he added kindly, "You don't want to take any notice of what the others say. They always rag new boys. Tell me about Shetland. Is it very different from here?"

They walked out into the playground and William, feeling he could trust Donald, began to tell him about Lerwick. Then he asked Donald about Aberdeen.

"Can you show me round the town?" he asked.

Donald, the son of a customs officer, seemed flattered that the new boy had accepted his offer of friendship. With him William gradually learnt his way about the streets, up and down the windy alleys, down to the fish quay from which the fish wives carried heavy baskets of fish up to the fishmarket at the end of Shiprow, and along the Castlegate, the focus of life on a market day, where lawyers and merchants congregated to discuss affairs. In cold weather they retreated to the warmth of the coffee house nearby, from where they would emerge in twos and threes in their tall hats and black coats, leaning on their canes and loath to go back to their offices and warehouses.

On a brisk frosty morning the boys, their cheeks glowing with the cold, would walk up two miles beyond Gallowgate to the quite separate town of old

Aberdeen, with its huddles of ivy-covered grey houses with their mossy roofs, up the High Street past King's College and its picturesque crown steeple, where they would catch sight of students in their red gowns passing to and fro. Or they might venture up beyond the Town House to where the canons' houses rose in their leafy gardens, to the magnificent St Machar's Cathedral and tiptoe inside to marvel at the size of the building and gaze at the blazons of Scottish families.

When the other boys at school realised that Donald had gone out of his way to befriend the new boy, and supported him on a number of occasions, some of them began to think that perhaps he was worth knowing, and they too began to make overtures of friendship. Within a few weeks William was accepted with the rest.

On Sundays the Macdonalds would attend the West Kirk of St Nicholas, often waiting till they heard the bells ring before setting off in the biting wind to sit shivering on hard pews listening to interminable sermons. William hated the dullness of the Scottish Sabbath and while he would seem to be staring up at the minister in his canopied pulpit, his thoughts would be elsewhere, perhaps with his sister whom he might see that afternoon when she and a friend would be coming to drink tea.

Margaret had been very sad and homesick at first, and missed her father dreadfully in spite of his fits of depression and sudden temper. It took her time after the company of her three brothers to get used to living among eighteen other young women, and being brought up to become a lady. She struggled with French though she felt that at home Dutch or Norwegian might be more practical. She became an accomplished needlewoman, learned to laugh and gossip, read, write and dream of a handsome husband. She looked forward to seeing her brother William, deemed "quite handsome" by one of her friends favoured with an invitation to the Macdonalds'. When she and William met they talked more often of their school life than of their lives at home in Shetland.

Letters from home came seldom and depended on the availability of the boats. It came as a shock to both of them when the term was well advanced, to receive a letter from their father in which he said that with the international situation and the winter weather he did not think it advisable for them to return to Shetland at the end of term. Therefore he was writing to Mr Macdonald and to the headmistress of Margaret's school asking them to make arrangements for his children to stay in Scotland over Christmas and Easter.

By now the winter weather was already more bitter than it usually was in Shetland, and the thought of missing out on Christmas and the New Year, and all the family and friendly visits they exchanged over that period to hearten the long dark days, made the two of them very miserable. Their only consolation was that their father seemed equally upset at the arrangements, to the extent of adding at the end of his letter: "I miss you both very much."

(4)

William discovered that there were other merchant families known to his father who invited him to take tea on Sunday afternoons and with whom he began to get friendly. One of them, Angus Maclean, was quite wealthy, and besides the house in Aberdeen where he lived during the winter months, also owned a property in the country where they retired to for a while in the summer.

William arrived at the Macleans' home for the first time with his sister Margaret and was impressed by the size of the stern grey house. A servant showed them into a wide entrance hall and ushered them into a drawing room full of elegantly carved furniture, a richly decorated carpet, engravings and oil paintings on the striped wallpaper and an air of culture and comfortable living. But if the sophistication of his surroundings made an impression on the boy, he was still more struck with Eleanor, the Macleans' eldest daughter, the same age as Margaret and a friend from her school. She was a little taller than he was, with a highly intelligent face, and a head of long dark-golden hair.

William had numbers of girl cousins and was not usually tongue-tied with girls. Eleanor was somehow different. He was so taken by her manner and looks that he did not know what to say. But she soon put him at his ease and asked him questions about Shetland. Soon they discovered plenty of things to talk about and when he left William looked forward to coming again. He felt flattered to be counted as Eleanor's friend.

Angus Maclean besides being a busy merchant talked of books, music and history and encouraged the young people to take an interest in the world about them. William noticed that the Macleans paid more attention to dress, took greater care in the preparation of food, were more distant to their servants than he was used to at home. When he went to their house there was always something exciting to talk about.

(5)

When he and Margaret finally returned at the end of June, the glorious days of the simmer dim had once again turned Shetland into a kind of paradise. Days when the sun hardly set, and silver evenings with seals sporting in the shining sea and birds wheeling overhead. Or there would be afternoons in Lerwick down by the harbour when the sea shone a bright blue and only the wide horizons and the pale vastness of the sky betrayed the fact that this was no southern sea. William and his sister had forgotten, or perhaps they had never been consciously aware, of the beauty of the Shetland landscape, where bare hillsides covered by peat and heather ended in valleys invaded by a loch or arm of the sea. From their summits you could see promontories and tiny islands and sometimes the land would end in gaunt grey cliffs around whose feet surged angry waves. High on the cliffs perched row upon row of guillemot and shag, Arctic terns swept by in the wind, and comical puffins with their red and yellow beaks darted past. All around were the huge herring gulls uttering their raucous cries. The landscape was untamed, rugged and unyielding with a beauty tinged with melancholy that tore at the heart. It was a beauty that had been engraved on William's mind from his earliest years, creating a bond with his native land that nothing would ever break.

Inevitably they had changed. Margaret was now growing into a tall and pretty young woman, and William had developed a sense of independence from living away from home. There was now a certain distance between them and their father. He no longer treated them as children but acknowledged their own different experience, and gave them little privileges denied to Andrew and James. Andrew was a headstrong boy envious of his brother and only longing for the time when he too could go south to school. Young James still clung to Aunt Grace who continued to look after them all.

Smuggling was more dangerous than ever now, and things were not going well for James. William grew critical of some of the things his father said and did. Since he had been away he looked on life almost as an outsider. He found he could flaunt his superior knowledge of the world to impress old friends who had not been to Aberdeen.

After the first reunions, when they were overjoyed to see their aunts, uncles, cousins and friends, to hear their own Shetland accent once again, and catch up on all that had happened during their absence, the summer passed quickly away. William appreciated even more the freedom to ride out on Shetland ponies, to go on business trips with his father, to enjoy the brief spells of fine weather going on long journeys by open boat.

At the same time, like sand dropping through an hour glass, his youth was slipping by, and all too soon came the time to take the boat and return, this time without James, with Margaret to Aberdeen. They were both dry-eyed and in eager conversation when James, who had gone with them in the skiff to see they boarded safely, kissed them solemnly on the cheek and climbed back down the rope ladder into his boat. He almost wanted to weep because his two eldest children were, like birds poised on the edge of the nest, almost ready to fly away.

William left the Grammar School when he was sixteen. The examinations were held in October in the presence of the whole school and members of the public, and William was very conscious that his brother Andrew, himself a gifted scholar, and their younger brother James, were among those assembled. To his surprise he did credit to himself and thus left the school on a wave of optimism. He was enrolled at King's College, and moved to old Aberdeen, to take up lodgings in the college and begin an entirely new life. Besides classes in classics and philosophy, there were visiting teachers to give instruction in dancing, French and bookkeeping. Meals were taken together in the college dining room and there were servants to wait on the young men.

There were other students there from the Grammar School, but there was a much greater freedom. The very day William moved into the college he was befriended by another new student called Richard, a tall, thin, sandy-haired youth whose father was a lawyer. He had the advantage of a few days' residence before William arrived, and showed him round the college buildings, and explained the routines of college life. For them both the world had no edges round it, and everything was new and exciting.

When lectures were over they would be free to wander, and would go down to the fish quay in Aberdeen and eye the fisher girls, tramp up to Fittie past the thick walls of the old blockhouse, now used as a boiling house for the production of whale oil, which gave off a terrible stench as they went by. There outside the huddle of cottages where the whalers lived they would see the enormous arches made of whitened whale jawbones, rising up in front of the gardens. One day they watched a whaling ship returning home. There was much rejoicing and they could hear the sailors singing a sea chanty as they came up the channel.

Some days they would go out and watch the building of the Aberdeen Canal, eventually to be eighteen miles long, and discuss how it was progressing. Along the river Dee they could see the dark-coloured sails of the fishing fleet as it sailed off on the high tide. What William liked best was to walk up the banks of the Dee along the quaysides where ships were loading and unloading. There they could see too the sheds and yards of the shipbuilders, smell the newly cut timber, and the odours of boiling tar and hemp. They could also talk to some of the men who worked there. It was a joy to see the shipbuilders and carpenters practising their centuries-old craft, sons of men who had not only built ships for generations, but had sailed in them too, to the northern coasts of Europe and the Arctic, trading, fishing and whaling. On one memorable occasion a weather-beaten bearded man had invited the young men into the yard and shown them the wooden model of the boat they were in the process of building. He explained to them in detail the woods used, how the decks were built and many other matters. William could scarcely tear himself away, as the whole atmosphere fascinated him.

Away from the Macdonalds' supervision, though he continued to visit them, William made other new friends, began to smoke a pipe, dabbled in gambling, sat up late drinking and singing, endlessly discussing life in theory. They all shared the inflated yet fragile confidence of adolescents with the world at their feet. William met other students from Marischal College, who were studying anatomy and physiology towards a medical degree and even visited the observatory that had been set up there. His horizons expanded, and he felt far removed from his brothers who were still in school.

(7)

One of the young men in William's circle who attracted his attention was a laird's son who dressed well and carried himself with a bit of a swagger. He was older and more sophisticated than William. One late evening William was passing through the quadrangle and in the pale glimmer of light coming from the porter's lodge caught sight of a figure he knew.

"Why, Jim, have you just come in?" he asked.

"I have just been down to Aberdeen," said Jim, somewhat wearily. "Do you think I can come and have a chat?"

Rumours had been going round that Jim was hopelessly in love with a beautiful fisherman's daughter from town. He was tall and handsome, and William admired him, not least because he had a mistress.

They went up to William's room and he lit a candle. Jim certainly did look anxious. William poured him a drink and they sat in the flickering light as Jim told his tale.

"You know I've got this girl, she's called Lizzie," he began. "I'm mad about her. Well, now she tells me she's pregnant – she's going to have my child. Whatever am I going to do?"

William was flattered to be taken into Jim's confidence, but he did not know what he could say. He had never envisaged this sort of predicament.

Jim went on, "I'd like to marry her," he said earnestly," but I don't think my parents will let me. Her father's a fisherman."

"What will you do?" asked William.

"I suppose I shall have to go and see them," said Jim groaning. "They won't be pleased to see me in the middle of term. They're already angry with me for being in debt. Why is life such a muddle?"

He tore his hand through his fine mop of dark curly hair and sighed.

A few days later a soberer chastened Jim re-appeared in college and there was no more talk of Lizzie. His parents had put their foot down and had threatened to disinherit him if he went ahead with the marriage.

"I had no chance," he told his friends. "If they cut me off I'm ruined for the rest of my life."

William secretly thought that he had already ruined Lizzie's young life. Jim was a scoundrel. Never again would he be taken in by appearances. His idol had fallen off his pedestal, leaving him wondering what he had seen in him in the first place.

(8)

Yet William was on the point of falling in love for the first time himself. It wasn't a fisher girl who had taken his fancy, but Angus Maclean's daughter Eleanor. Margaret, William's sister, had by now returned to Shetland, but William still visited the Macleans' house. He had not really paid Eleanor any more attention than he usually paid to his sister's friends, though he had always felt there was something special about her. But now he was learning to dance and was being sought after to join in the Macleans' social evenings held at their big house. Anyone seeing them together would say that they made a handsome pair, he tall, dark and with a certain grace, she with a pale pink complexion and a beautiful head of golden hair. They would dance with a swirl of kilts and long dresses to fiddles and sometimes the bagpipes, and as Eleanor enthusiastically clapped her hands at the end of a dance, he suddenly saw her in a new light. The way she smiled made him feel tall, and when he got home he found himself picturing her face, her dress, her smile. Then he began to wait anxiously for another occasion when he could see her, even inventing excuses to call at her father's house in order to catch a glimpse of her. She always seemed pleased to see him, but he wondered whether she had any particular feelings for him. He agonised over whether he should tell her how he felt, but the opportunity never seemed to arise, and in any case he didn't seem to know how to begin. His studies began to seem arid and pointless compared to the excitement he experienced when he saw her, and he was seriously wondering about confiding in his friend Richard and asking his advice.

It was at this point, after William had been at King's for about a year, that a letter came from home which shattered all his plans and turned his life upside down.

He glanced at the letter eagerly, always pleased to have news from his father. But he noticed at once that it wasn't in his father's hand. He tore open the seal and unfolded the doubled-up sheet of paper.

The letter was from Aunt Grace.

"My dearest William," it began. "I am writing to you at the earliest opportunity but I can't be sure how soon you will receive my news. I'm afraid it will come as a shock to you and your brothers, and I don't know how to prepare you for it. Your father has suffered a very severe breakdown and his health is very much impaired. He weeps and tells us he hears voices and is altogether unable to carry on with business at the moment. I think it was brought on by the death of your grandfather in Yell – he was of course buried by the time the letter reached us – but your father could not seem to accept it and it shattered him completely. I've never seen him in such a pitiable state.

"William, he asks constantly for you. As his eldest son and heir he looks to you for support and although I keep him company and attend to all his needs as best I can, you are the only person who can help him. I am at the end of my tether to know what to do. Your Uncle Charles Ogilvy has been here and we have discussed the matter. I implore you to endeavour to come home to Lerwick as soon as you can get a ship. Your father has money in the Commercial Bank and you can draw on the bank for whatever you need. William, I fear you will have to abandon all idea of further studies at the moment and settle your mind to helping your father's business, though I know that is not what you really wanted. I hope that the thought that you are sorely needed here will help to soften the blow. Please come as soon as you can. Your loving aunt Grace."

The full impact of the letter did not hit him when he first read it. Instead, somewhat stunned, he put it in his pocket and determined to return straightaway to the college. For once thoughts of Eleanor had been banished by events of a more solemn nature. His heart beating fast, he covered the two miles up to the college in record time and heard a clamour of young voices coming from the quadrangle. But at this moment he wanted to be alone and slipped unnoticed into the dusty gothic chapel, sat on the edge of one of the carved oak stalls and pulled out the letter again. In the dim light that filtered through the windows it was difficult to read. However he needed to take it all in and decide what he was going to do.

Life had been very pleasant since he had been at King's. It had offered so many new opportunities, so many new windows on the world. It was like being on the crest of a wave. Now suddenly that wave had crashed. There was to be no more college life for him, no more friends, no more parties, no more days at liberty wandering round Aberdeen. He would have to go back to Lerwick, where the people were fine, but where everyone knew everyone else and horizons were more limited. Just now he was getting a taste for the finer things of life and wondering if with a degree he might enter one of the professions and lead a different sort of life from his father. Then there was Eleanor. He would have to leave her behind and maybe when he came back she would have another young man. He wondered whether he would ever come back, and if he did, whether things would ever be the same.

He sat for a long while in the gloom with a very heavy heart. The chapel was seldom used and his emotions were too shaken for him consciously to pray. Yet strangely enough, when finally he got up to leave, his mind was more at ease because he had already courageously taken several important decisions.

He would go down to the harbour again tomorrow and discover the earliest passage he could get to Lerwick. He would have to tell Andrew and James about their father. He would go to the bank and withdraw some money, settle any debts and pack his belongings together. He would have to tell Richard and other friends in the college of his decision. He would call on the Macdonalds to say farewell. And as soon as possible he would go to say goodbye to Eleanor. He had gone into the chapel a weak-kneed boy. He came out just as heavy hearted, but transformed into a man.

(10)

There was something especially poignant about going to visit the Macleans' house. He took in every detail as he had never done before, conscious of the fact that he might never come again. As he waited for Eleanor to arrive in the drawing room with its white marble fireplace, dark paintings and striped wallpaper, he felt as if he were watching another person act out the scene. He was facing the window and looked round as she entered, in a powder-blue dress that rustled as she moved, and looking flushed and beautiful after a walk. Her mother, a strikingly good-looking woman whom Eleanor closely resembled, greeted William like an old friend, and went out of the room, leaving them together.

"How nice to see you," Eleanor began, friendly as usual, sitting down and gesturing to him to join her. But he remained standing.

"Why, you look as if you had seen a ghost!" she exclaimed. "Is something the matter?"

"Eleanor, I have had some very serious news from home," he began, going straight to the point. "My father is very ill and my aunt says there's nothing for it but for me to go home directly and carry on the business."

"But isn't there anyone else?" cried Eleanor at once. "How long will you be gone? And your studies?"

"I'm the eldest son," said William gravely, spelling out the responsibility he had so recently acknowledged to himself. "It's got to be me."

"Then I shan't see you for ages," said Eleanor, betraying a very real concern. "When will you come back?"

"I don't know when I shall come back," said William. "And I doubt if I shall go back to college."

"You mean we shan't see each other again?" whispered Eleanor.

"Will you mind?" began William.

"I shall mind very much," said Eleanor.

William felt very tempted to tell her how he felt about her, but somehow as he was going away forever he decided it didn't seem fair. So he smiled nobly and sat down and they talked of this and that without really getting to reveal their true feelings.

At last he got up to go.

Impulsively he blurted out," Eleanor, I shall never forget you," bent down and kissed her gently on the cheek. Then without another word he hastily left the room, leaving Eleanor flushed and with tears in her eyes. Not feeling that he could trust his own composure, he bade Mrs Maclean a less than courteous farewell, and escaped as soon as he could into the street.

(11)

It was a fine day when he left. Mr Macdonald and his wife, and both his brothers came down to the quayside to see him off. He remembered vividly the first day he had arrived in Aberdeen, then so strange, now so familiar. He remembered how it had felt when his father had returned to Shetland and he had been left alone. And now he was alone once again, and leaving Aberdeen not knowing when if ever he would be back.

The journey was the most painful he had ever undertaken. One part of him wanted to get back to Shetland as quickly as possible, but the other was fearful of what he would find and wanted to prolong the getting there. Soon after leaving Aberdeen and the safety of the harbour they were chased by a French ship and for a short while the prospect of further dangers and excitements banished William's preoccupations from his mind. Fortunately a navy cutter appeared on the horizon and made rapidly for the French ship, which beat a retreat and finally disappeared eastwards into the North Sea. Round the north of Scotland the sea was very rough, and down below William and the other passengers were thrown mercilessly from side to side. Next morning south of

Sumburgh Head the waters were turbulent and it was not until they reached Bressay Sound that they encountered relative calm. A grey sea and a grey sky greeted them. The decks stank of cattle, but the air was fresh, and a light mist hung over Lerwick as the ship hove to in the harbour. A mixture of emotions stirred within William, the grey buildings huddled round the harbour, and the fort up on the hill, the thought of home and of folk he loved always moved him when he returned. Now however, things would be different. What did the future hold for him now?

CHAPTER THREE

Apprenticeship

When he arrived home William was taken aback to see how his father had altered. He looked older, pale, tired and abstracted, got up very late and did very little. Although he had seemed pleased to see his son, flinging his arms round him and holding him close in a way William never remembered during recent years, it was obvious that he was to be disturbed as little as possible and a pall of anxiety hung over the household. Margaret was at home, and seemed to have more say in running the house, and this was a blessing, because William could talk to her of people they knew in Aberdeen, though he did not mention his love for Eleanor. His Aunt Grace treated him kindly and with far more respect than he remembered, and now asked his advice on various family matters. William began to realise what an important figure in his life his father was, and how he relied on him even when he was away. Now James had abdicated his position and this left an enormous gap in all their lives. What if he had died? To William it seemed as if he had always been living in a kind of dream world, and now he had somehow suddenly hit reality. And this reality was painful, although at the same time it was something he could face head on, unlike the vague fears he had entertained during the voyage home. It was stressful at first for life had changed, while his surroundings, the rest of his family and the unusually beautiful summer weather constantly reminded him of happier times.

For the last year or two James had been in partnership with a man called Basil Spence, who with the help of Charles Ogilvy had kept things ticking over. But there was a lot of business to be done in connection with cargoes of timber and arranging for stocks of cured fish to be shipped south, and soon after he returned William went down to the warehouse, and spent the afternoon in the counting-house trying to make sense of the accounts. As James' eldest son he was familiar with the general outline of the business, and knew some of the people involved, but now in a very short time he had to take some positive action and assume new responsibilities.

He could see that James' affairs were in something of a muddle. He obviously did a lot of business by word of mouth, by personal visits and private arrangements. William sat himself down at the table in the tiny counting house, and once he was alone lent his head on his arms on the table and felt like weeping. What use were all his Latin and Greek to him now? All that learning wasted! Yet how ill equipped he felt to tackle a practical job, something that his father with less education had at his fingertips. There was humiliation mingled with his desperation. All at once he remembered what his school headmaster had said all those years ago; "Classics, it lifts the mind to higher things." But the higher things William had thought he meant now seemed to be beyond his grasp.

It was no use regretting the past. The present situation had to be confronted with as much courage as he could muster. Deliberately he seized the daybook, turned to the beginning of the year, and began reading his father's correspondence in his spiky copperplate hand. He read until late in the evening and his head ached, for the light summer evening made him forget the time.

(2)

William didn't miss his life in Aberdeen in a conscious way at first. He felt in fact as if he had suddenly moved on beyond his college friends, that in this crisis he was being challenged to live authentically for the first time. He had a tremendous amount to learn in a short while, and he discovered that his father had done nearly everything for himself: he oversaw the store, checked the accounts, wrote the letters, met the fish curers and the lairds, arranged for the transport of fish, set prices, was in charge of the cargo boats when they left and when they returned, dealt with all the ships' masters. He had it all in his head. He also had a network of people he dealt with in both England and Scotland whom he visited regularly.

One night after William had eaten at Uncle Thomas' house and the two of them were drinking tea afterwards, William voiced his doubts as to whether he would ever really be able to help his father.

"You have to be absolutely honest and trustworthy," said his uncle. "That's the first rule. A merchant also needs to be able to get on with people, choose the right friends, and of course, never stop work."

William was about to break in when his uncle continued; "I sometimes think that your father drives himself too hard. Look what he's achieved. He's bought land and other property, and ships – he'd have a tidy fortune if it weren't always at the mercy of the sea and the weather. And don't worry because you can't do everything at once. We all have to learn some time, though I think your father would have done better to send you to another merchant's house to learn the job. That's what I did."

34

As summer drew to a close and the autumn approached, James seemed to take a turn for the better. One morning, much to William's surprise, he came down to the warehouse and stayed to talk, as if suddenly anxious to see how things were going. From then on he would appear every day, and began to look himself again, even planning to travel south. Aunt Grace confided to William that she thought having him and his two brothers back from school for the summer had done him good. William caught a look of relief on her face as she watched James entertaining a couple of officers from the garrison in the old way.

William too began to relax. The tense concentration with which he had gone about his tasks gave way to a mood of boredom and listlessness. He began to miss his more exciting life in Aberdeen. As his father slowly began to resume his normal pattern of work, William found things even more difficult. James had been used to doing things his own way, and although he was grateful to his son for coming home, William had tried to do everything differently. In addition he made what James felt were errors of judgement. At this stage William felt rebellious, and no longer ready to accept criticism from his father.

One morning at home James reiterated something he should have done which had been a sore point with William the day before, and he began angrily to make excuses. James' temper flared up, and when he shouted at him, William could bear it no longer.

"You've no right to treat me like this," he stormed, and raised his hand as if to strike his father. But James reacted more quickly, and hit his son full in the face. Both immediately recoiled in horror. William stood there dazed, blood trickling from his nose. Very pale, James turned and strode out of the room.

(3)

Now the worst had happened. His father had actually struck him in anger. At first William boiled with hatred, to think that he should have done such a thing to his own son. He staggered to a chair, feeling faint, and tried to mop his face. The house seemed to have gone terribly quiet. As the minutes passed William's mood changed. He wanted his father to come and ask his forgiveness. He even began to feel sorry for him, because he had been ill. Still nobody came. Then at last Aunt Grace came in quietly and put her arm round him.

"Why, what a mess," she exclaimed and ran off for damp cloths. "Here," she said to the maid. "He's had a nosebleed. Just leave us alone will you."

"I think it has hurt him as much as it has hurt you," she said. "He's never gone that far. You must try to forgive him."

Nothing more was said when Margaret came to find William but he suspected she knew what had happened. And it was going to be difficult to explain away the black eye that had come up all blue and raw. Things were tense for the rest of the day.

Next morning James himself took the initiative and stood before William as if he didn't know what to say.

"Father," said William impulsively, going to him and laying his head on his shoulder.

"I shouldn't have done it," began James.

"I shouldn't have threatened you," whispered William.

They sat down at the table.

"But we can't go on as we are," said James. "I've been thinking about you all night. I have written a letter to my friend Robert Bell in Hull asking him to arrange for both you and Andrew to do a merchant apprenticeship there. It's something I've had in mind for some time. Hull's the largest fishing port in the kingdom and has the biggest whaling fleet. It's the best I can do for you. When you are back we can work as partners; I shall need your help. I've lots of ideas for the future. I can't do it alone. Will you agree?"

William looked at his father's flushed face and pleading eyes. His own eye was still half shut and it hurt. But through it all he knew that deep down he still loved his father.

He hesitated. Then, "Yes," he said, "I will."

(4)

It was autumn when after an exhausting journey south by ship, William arrived in Hull. His first impressions were blurred by tiredness. He remembered seeing the citadel near the entrance to the harbour and then entering the river with its rows of solid red-brick warehouses several stories high on the west bank, a customs-house and an array of small vessels moored along the quayside. Then as the ship nosed its way forward they slipped along the canal and under the lifting bridge into the dock and finally pulled in alongside a tall masted whaling ship. Porters swarmed onto the deck but William hesitated. He had expected to be met at the ship but while many people crowded on deck to claim their loved ones, no one seemed to be on the look-out for him. His heart sank. Here he was in England for the first time and there was no welcome. It did not promise well. He tried to reassure himself, squaring his shoulders and staring round at the crowded dock and its busy hum of activity, and at the seagulls circling overhead who seemed to be mocking his arrival. In any case he wanted to go ashore and summoned one of the few remaining porters to take his trunk.

"Where to?" he asked.

"Take me to the inn on the High Street," said William. "I have to call on a gentleman there."

They were just about to depart when a man in black rode up and hastily dismounted. He was short and plump with a slightly balding head. He hurried towards William.

"William Hay?" he asked a little breathlessly. "I apologise for my late appearance. Important business took me out of Hull and I have only just received news of your ship's arrival. I am John Fryer. I know your father well. Welcome to Hull."

William shook his hand vigorously with a feeling of relief.

"You must be tired after your journey," said Mr Fryer. "We've been looking forward to your coming. But I expect you'd like to settle in at the inn. It's the King's Head. It's not far from my business. I'll take you there myself. Then I'll leave you to relax and we can see each other again tomorrow morning."

They set off through a maze of narrow paved streets and down a twisting lane which proved to be the High Street. To their left were gabled houses of red brick with wide facades onto the street, houses of considerable dignity, and on the other a number of older jettied timber-framed houses with ornate carvings. In between the houses to the east William glimpsed the river down some narrow alleyways. All around him was an atmosphere of well-being and ease.

"My business is just along there across the road," said Mr Fryer, smiling and patting his horse as they arrived at the inn, and the porter who had been following them delivered the trunk. "Nowadays I live up on the other side of the dock. There's more space there for my family and it's pleasanter to live away from the warehouse. I hope at the weekend you will come and meet my family. I'll leave you now to find your room and have a meal. I'll see you at the counting-house tomorrow."

Waving his hand in a friendly gesture, he left William to go into the inn.

(5)

After a generous meal and a good night's sleep, William woke refreshed. He saw that it was a bright October day and still surprisingly warm. As soon as he came downstairs he heard the servants' unfamiliar Yorkshire accent and remembered that he was in England. As he ate his breakfast, he felt eager to begin his new life.

Outside the High Street was already busy with all manner of carriers and carts, wagons, horses and ponies. He reached Mr Fryer's business early, conscious of having taken special pains over his appearance. The redbrick double-fronted house had three stories and stood slightly back from the street, fenced off by iron railings. A large signboard, JOHN FRYER hung across under the eaves. William climbed the two steps up to the front door and pulled the bell, his heart beating a little faster than usual. After a moment a young man not much older than he was opened the door.

"I'm William Hay," began William in his unfamiliar accent. "Mr Fryer is expecting me."

"Mr Fryer won't be here yet. But please come in. I'm Paul Smith. I'm his clerk. I'll show you your desk and some of the books. Peter, the other clerk, is not here yet."

He ushered William into the roomy hall, up the wide staircase with its shiny polished balustrade and into an office that looked out over the High Street. From the window William could catch sight of the inn-sign of the inn where he was staying.

There was a large desk with a leather-covered chair, three separate benches with tall shiny stools, shelves with numerous leather-bound books, shiny inkwells, quill pens, and a pewter mug.

"We trade mainly with the Baltic in hemp and flax," explained Paul as they sat down. He took some of the books down from the shelf.

"These are all details of all the goods that have come into our warehouse, whether by land or sea. And these," he said, "are all our customers' invoices. They all have to be entered into the ledgers. Then there are all the cashbooks, receipts and payments, money paid out from the bank or paid in. We have to balance the cash and calculate cash-in-hand every month. The accounts are settled up on December 1st. It's a hard job because the afternoons draw in and the mornings are dark and you're working by candlelight. Then this," he picked up another fat book, "is the bill book. Every detail is recorded here of each bill of exchange, when it was received, by whom it was drawn, and where; to whom it was paid away and when it matures. And at the back of the book, look, there are our own acceptances, bills other people draw on us. When they fall due they all have to be honoured."

"There's a lot to do here," commented William, his Shetland accent contrasting strangely with Paul's.

"That's only the beginning," said Paul. "There are the sales books, and the warehouse book, and all the carriage and freight charges have to be written up in the daybook. And this," taking down a huge book, "this is where we paste all the invoices of purchases."

"And letterbooks," queried William, beginning to have misgivings about all the work he would have to learn.

"These are the letterbooks," said Paul proudly, pointing to a row of thick volumes on the shelf. "We write every letter clearly into the letterbook — you are always expected to copy every letter out in full, even if you think it is not important. Mr Fryer insists. And then there are all the copies of letters to be made ready to send off. All the letters that come to us we keep for seven years. Some of them contain news about political matters, movements of ships and so on that can help us in our business."

It took Paul some time to explain to William what was in the books, and William knew that it would probably take him ages before he knew how to deal with all of them. He would have to learn how to establish buying and selling prices, to deal with exchange rates, to convert weights and measures, to work out simple and compound interest, to cope with all the various sources of credit and be able to draw up a balance sheet.

Shortly after ten o'clock they heard the door below open and a brisk step on the stairs, and Mr Fryer looked in to see William's dark and Paul's fair heads bent together over a letterbook.

"I'm glad to see you are so keen to get down to business," he said with a smile. "But you know, a merchant does not spend all his time in his counting-house. And you haven't seen the warehouse where my goods are stored yet. But first of all I want to show you this fine city of ours. We merchants are proud of our heritage here. We're going to leave Paul to get on with today's correspondence and I'm taking you out to see Hull."

(6)

"We've got the largest fishing fleet in the world here," said Mr Fryer, as they set off. "Over 300 ships. And an impressive whaling fleet. We import a lot of goods and it's we merchants who have made this place what it is. Let's go down to the harbour."

First they walked down one of the tiny alleyways between the house and the next one.

"We call these pathways 'staithes' here in Yorkshire," Mr Fryer explained. "They all lead down to the quayside."

Nearby small coasting vessels were loading and unloading, and other small boats were moored further out. The sun shone brightly over the water as they walked down past the wharves and warehouses behind the houses in the High Street.

"That tall warehouse belongs to Mr Summers," said Mr Fryer. "He's a corn merchant. They are loading grain just now." They watched as the dust rose as the grain was poured into the hold.

"Some of the merchants who trade here are of course very wealthy," he continued as they walked on. "A merchant's reputation depends on two things – his character and his wealth. It's all a matter of prompt payment. You can't afford to let people down, because if you do they won't trust you, and it's all a matter of trust."

Further on he pointed to another warehouse and said, " The man who owns this warehouse is also a wealthy whaling merchant. There are whaling ships laid up for the winter in the dock. Let's go down there now."

They turned left at the end of the High Street and soon found themselves by the dock. First William saw the dock office and the lifting bridge over the canal, and beyond, the masts of sailing ships and the sails of a windmill silhouetted against the blue sky. Nearby was the tower of a church, and building yards where ships' masts were being built. Mr Fryer fascinated William by telling him about all the facilities the dock offered.

"But this dock is not large enough for all the ships that want to use it," he said. "They are planning to build another one."

As they passed the whaling ships, Mr Fryer explained how five of them had been lost the year before.

"We made five separate collections in aid of the seamen and their families."

William ventured to say that whaling ships called in regularly at Lerwick and explained that the whalers tended to go on a spending spree when they came back and got drunk.

"Well, it's a hard life," said Mr Fryer. "One of these ships was caught in the ice last year and had to winter in the Arctic. Of course, I believe you have been in Aberdeen. I wondered just now why you hadn't commented on the smell of the Greenland yards where they boil the blubber," he said. "It hangs over the whole of town, especially in the summer. And that's why most of us who can afford it have removed from the High Street. You want to get away from it. The really rich merchants live outside Hull. We live a little to the north of here. You'll see when you come to visit us."

They wandered back down Lowgate to the newly rebuilt Market Place and finally past the splendid brick church of Holy Trinity in the centre of town. Compared to the hilly streets of Aberdeen, Hull was almost flat and thickly populated. William felt exhilarated in the bustle of such a large town. From being apprehensive he began to look forward to the future with eagerness.

(7)

All the same, those first few months, living in the inn and working in the counting-house, were hard. Long hours working on the different tasks from eight in the morning and sometimes when business was brisk, till eight in the evening by flickering candlelight. William's eyes burned and his back ached, and his fingers were stained with ink, and he realised that working for his father, and still more working with his father, had not been the same. He was used to study, but he had never really submitted to the demands of a job. It was hard, leaving university in Aberdeen where he had had every freedom, to accept that he had to do what someone else asked him, whether he felt like it or not. The work itself exacted a certain strict discipline: it had to be done well, and finished on time. William realised that his father, in spite of his criticisms, had made excuses for him and covered up for his mistakes. Here Mr Fryer was a stern master with high standards. But he was perfectly fair, and while he might pull him up sharply he also gave him credit for work well done. Nor did he fly into sudden rages like his father.

"Mr Fryer's a good person to work for," confided Paul one day, and Peter, a lanky, fair-haired youth, agreed. "Only you have to earn his respect."

There was a curious smell about the warehouse where the piles of flax were unloaded. Outside Scandinavian ships moored at the wharf to unload. Sometimes William had the chance to talk to the ships' masters.

The hardest job, as Paul had predicted, was getting the books ready for December 1st. Some days no column of figures would seem to add up the same upwards as downwards, and it was with an air of rejoicing that they announced that it was done. Mr Fryer himself checked their results, and said he was satisfied with the profit they had made that year. He insisted they all drink a glass of red wine to celebrate. It was with relief that William realised that he had passed the first part of his apprenticeship.

(8)

From now on it was not only the most tedious tasks that fell to William's lot. He was taken by Mr Fryer to other merchants' warehouses; to visit ships as they arrived in dock; to inspect samples; to listen to Mr Fryer deliberating on prices, insurance, freight, shipping and other matters. Mr Fryer spent a lot of time discussing affairs with other merchants, reading the financial news in the papers, and sending and receiving letters from other merchants in other parts of the country so that he could judge as to the best time to dispose of his goods and at what price.

William clearly remembered the first time he was involved in a deal. Mr Fryer had sat the evening before explaining to William what he hoped to achieve.

"You give away just a little at a time," he said, "and only if you are forced to. And just when your business partner thinks he's done a brilliant deal, you bring out your trump card."

When the visiting merchant arrived he was taken to dine at the nearby inn, in a manner William was quite unused to, and then they repaired to the warehouse. In a large room with a big table in the centre they sat down and began to puff out little whirls of smoke from their cigars. Then they began to talk. William remembered perfectly everything that was said, though no one took any notes.

"I've come to you because you have a reputation for being fair," began Mr Wright, a big, florid man with a fair moustache. "I've had very little luck this year with the linen side of my manufacturing business. I believe you can supply flax from Sweden. What's the likelihood of your being able to supply me with flax this spring?"

"Well, that depends on what you want," began Mr Fryer cautiously. "There are various qualities and prices. How much are you looking for?"

"Well, about twenty bales initially I think."

"That should be no problem. I have several contacts both in Sweden and in Norway. And when do you need them?"

"Let's say by Easter."

"And your wagons would load here at my warehouse," pursued Mr Fryer. "The ship freight would be mine, the land freight yours."

"And the insurance to be shared."

"Will you personally see to the carriage?"

"A colleague of mine, Mr Rochester, has other business in Hull. I shall leave him to organise that."

Mr Fryer suddenly frowned

"Let me see, Rochester, haven't we already had some dealings with him, in Huddersfield I think? William, bring me the accounts, there is something I want to check."

William fetched the big account book and was fortunately able to quickly track down an earlier account with Mr Rochester.

He hesitated.

"It hasn't been paid," he said, a little embarrassed.

Mr Wright went a little pale.

"I have to admit that I have not known him for very long," he said. His tone suggested that he knew that the deal was over. "Only a matter of six months."

"Mr Wright, this causes me some concern," said Mr Fryer. "I must give it some thought. I'll be in touch."

There was no rudeness but coolness had crept into the air. After a few more general remarks to cover up his confusion, Mr Wright got up to leave.

When he had gone Mr Fryer turned to William.

"I'm glad you could find those entries, William. Now you can see just how careful you have to be. Never trust a man until you know whom he deals with. There are plenty of shady dealers around. You can't afford to make even one mistake. Always remember that."

(9)

There were many new experiences for William to face during his first year in Hull. The unfamiliar flat countryside and the size of the town made him miss the bare hillsides of Shetland and the little town of Lerwick. It was difficult to get used to living among Englishmen, whose customs and ways of thinking were different from his. At first he felt homesick and ill at ease. Although frequent travellers passing to and fro made the inn a bustling place, he often felt lonely because most of them were much older than he was and had their own business to attend to. It was the first time in his life he had lived independently, and there was many an evening when, exhausted with work and study he hastily finished his meal and crept up to his room, longing for the companionship of his family in Shetland or his friends in Aberdeen. He was aware of a difference between himself and his two fellow clerks, because he had been to university and they had not.

After a while his willingness and good humour broke down the barriers, and Paul and Peter became good friends. From discussing problems at work they went on to talking about themselves, their home-life and families and the differences between living in Shetland and Yorkshire.

Eventually Peter invited William home to meet his parents and young sister Amelia. The Thatchers ran a watermill on the outskirts of Hull. They lived in part of the tall warehouse with the constant sound of the millrace in their ears. It was Sunday lunchtime and an aunt and uncle and their daughter Anne, the same age as Amelia, made up the party.

William was soon put at ease by their warmth and jollity, and enjoyed the Yorkshire pudding, roast beef and puddings he was offered. Amelia and Anne giggled and blushed when William spoke to them. Then they became bolder and asked him questions about where he came from.

"What do you do in Shetland during the long dark winters then?" they asked, and he told them Shetlanders were praised for their hospitality and friendliness and enjoyed dancing, singing, feasting and visiting each others' houses.

Flattered that William should have had such success with the young ladies, Peter reclaimed his attention for himself. He had dreams of going to London and he and William walked out along the river during the afternoon and talked about plans for the future. William always looked back to that invitation with gratitude. It was the first time he felt at ease among strangers. Other invitations followed.

William also enjoyed Mr Fryer's hospitality at the weekend, and grew to admire him, for he was a man of great integrity, a regular worshipper at Holy Trinity church, a good father and an openhearted citizen. His home was in a relatively new street to the north-west of the dock and he had a large number of lively children, the eldest not a lot younger than Andrew, and an engaging wife who kept house with the help of several servants. They were a happy household and Mr Fryer soon changed from being a stern master to being a caring friend. He took an interest in a wide range of public affairs and talked to William about the textile factories he had visited in both Yorkshire and Lancashire, and expressed deep concern about the way in which in some of them women and children were being exploited. He hated the unhealthy conditions in which people were forced to live in these industrial towns, which had sprung up in the last thirty years, without any planning, where the vestry government couldn't cope and the Church had not enough clergy or resources to minister to them. And then there was the Slave Trade, making merchants in places like Bristol and Liverpool immensely rich at the expense of poor black slaves.

"It's important to care about these matters," he told William one day, when other visitors had expressed the view that there was nothing anyone could do. "One day justice will be done and the whole wicked system will be abolished."

As William got to know Mr Fryer better, and some of his fellow merchants in Hull whom he met in the course of business, he began to have a different idea of a merchant's calling. His father had failed to give him a vocation. But here was a man he admired, whom he wanted to imitate, and whose interest and friendship he cherished. He began to lose his negative attitudes and to build-up new goals for himself and standards by which to conduct his life.

Through Mr Fryer he was occasionally invited to social evenings, dances or concerts where he met other merchants and their friends, and sometimes their daughters. But although this attractive dark Shetlander aroused attention, in his own mind there was no one quite like Eleanor. Perhaps he was too occupied with pressure of work and a new life to lose his heart again so soon. Or perhaps he was secretly afraid to allow himself to be mastered again by such powerful emotions. He was flattered by their attentions but no one seemed to compare with Eleanor. He thought wistfully of her in Aberdeen and wondered whether she ever thought of him.

(10)

When he had been in Hull for nearly a year, William's brother Andrew joined him. He came to live with another merchant called Mr Simon who lived in a large mansion on the outskirts of Hull. It had all been arranged through the good offices of Mr Fryer. William had looked forward eagerly to his brother's arrival, to have someone he could talk to about life at home, but right from the start their different situations created competition between the brothers. There were other areas of jealousy. Andrew was very good at figures, and dealing with the accounts of a prosperous merchant was a prospect he relished. Moreover, while William was working hard and gaining some small credit with Mr Fryer, Andrew soon found he had a real flair for buying and selling and for driving a hard bargain. He was soon in Mr Simon's favour and was promoted very quickly to greater responsibilities. Instead of enjoying Andrew's company William felt undervalued and very much in his shadow, in spite of being the elder brother. He had been in Hull a year longer and already his brother was outshining him.

Matters came to a head when Mr Fryer, no doubt hoping to cause William pleasure, remarked, "William, your brother will go far."

William turned later to Andrew and said almost savagely, "How does it come about that you are everybody's favourite?"

Andrew, quite unaware of any feelings he might have aroused, looked surprised.

"How do you mean?" he asked.

"Well, everything you do seems to be one big success. You've only been here a short while and Mr Simon's promoted you. And you haven't been living in an inn like I have. I've had a real struggle to get where I am. You just take it all for granted."

Andrew was not James Hay's son for nothing. He was used to his father's sudden inexplicable changes of mood and depression. William seemed to share his father's oversensitive emotions. This was not he first time he had sensed his elder brother's jealousy toward him. Secure in himself and in his success, he was prepared to be generous.

"Maybe I've been lucky," he said, in an attempt to reassure his brother. Then he added, "William, never forget that Father wants you to go home and work with him. James and I will have to make our own way in the world."

In due course, William's apprenticeship came to an end, and he returned to Shetland, on the threshold of a new life.

CHAPTER FOUR

Changes

B ack in Shetland several years later, on a bright spring morning in May, William was riding on a Shetland pony up the track that led through the Tingwall valley. High fluffy clouds cast dappled and ever-changing shadows over the yellow hills, reflected in the empty stretches of water, and seemed to be part of the open, treeless landscape. Here and there near the track patches of primroses shone in the sunlight and the breeze was mild. Topping a rise William came upon a couple of women, still young and both of them barefoot, carrying tall baskets on their backs and knitting as they went. Behind them trudged a man carrying over his shoulder a narrow iron spade which was used for breaking clods and cutting peats. William called out a greeting and they replied cheerfully but with respect.

When they had gone his mind slipped back to the times he had spent in England and he compared the poverty of his Shetland people to the relative affluence of workers in Hull. The agricultural workers in the villages in Yorkshire had been poor enough but even they had shoes to wear. Yet the Shetlanders weren't downtrodden, they were friendly and hospitable, and it felt good to be back amongst his own people. Although he now was travelling further afield on his father's business and becoming a man of the world.

William was now twenty-three. After returning from Hull he had begun working with his father and assuming more responsibility for the business. Relationships with his father had healed, James had mellowed and William was more mature. Business was doing well and William began to see great opportunities ahead of him. On this fine spring morning with the sun quite warm and the curlews piping, he felt that the world was good, and he was happy with his lot.

Just then he came in sight of Tingwall church and the grey stone manse, and reached the short stretch of road which the minister, the Reverend Turnbull, had had built. The glebe property was enclosed, not by the usual turf-built fences, but by drystone walls, and the few crofts together that made up the village looked tidy and well tended. As he approached the manse the Mr Turnbull himself appeared at the door, a dapper, white-haired figure in black, and beckoning William in with a wave of the hand and a cheery smile, invited him to have a drink.

"Business going well?" enquired the minister, as he poured William a glass of brandy.

"The lodberry is nearly finished," replied William, referring to the larger house with its warehouse jutting out into Bressay Sound that James had recently had built south of the Tolbooth. "Father's going to build a pier so that the boats can tie up. Now that he's got several boats going up to the haaf stations, we need more space. He has it in mind to get other ships, and even to buy land and set up curing stations for himself."

"Your father's an ambitious man," remarked Mr Turnbull. "He's done a great deal for the neighbourhood, encouraging the expansion of Lerwick and building up the fishing trade. I know in the past he tried to set up a fairer system, with the fishermen being paid for what they catch and sharing the ownership of their boats. But as you must realise, here in Shetland the lairds have had it all their own way; they make whatever profit they can and the men, well, they are exploited."

"But things must change," said William earnestly, with the optimism of youth.

"It'll be a bold man who challenges the hold of the lairds," said the minister. "But the world is changing. If we ever win this dreary war, I think things will be different. Maybe you younger men will have a better chance. Although I don't approve of the Revolution and the Terror they had in France, I understand from what I've read that the lives of the peasants have drastically changed."

"Our folk are so poor," said William. "They have so little, I always took it for granted."

After a pause he added, "This is good brandy Mr Turnbull."

"That's a gift from your father," said Mr Turnbull with a twinkle in his eye. "No questions as to where it comes from."

"I never thought you as a minister would condone smuggling."

"Well, it's another of those aspects of life up here that don't seem to change," replied Mr Turnbull. "Sometimes you have to turn a blind eye."

"I've never known anything else," admitted William. "Just now I'm beginning to have qualms."

"You won't get much sympathy from your father," said the minister, "or from Charles Ogilvy. Has he settled down with his new wife? And how's the rest of your family?"

William began explaining that Andrew and James were soon to join a merchant firm in Liverpool, importing timber from New Brunswick.

"They've got their own careers to make," said Mr Turnbull. "It's sad how all our young men have to leave Shetland. But I maintain that every Shetlander who goes away leaves part of his heart behind. And what about your sister Margaret? Am I to believe the rumour that she's getting engaged to the laird's son from Busta? It could be a good match for her."

Mr Turnbull was a warm-hearted man who took a genuine interest in his parishioners and received their affection in return. At the same time he loved to discuss local affairs with all the people that mattered and items of more general importance with his visitors. After chatting a while longer he told William he had business to attend to and William got up to go.

"The summer will soon be here," said Mr Turnbull. "Let's hope we get a good year for the crops. I'm experimenting with a rotation system using turnips. This is the most fertile valley in the whole of Shetland. If it doesn't work here, it's unlikely to be a success anywhere else. Tell your father I intend to ride over to see him at the end of the week. He's not much of a one for religion but now he's got an estate of his own he's interested in agriculture and he enjoys a good chat. Give him my regards."

"I will tell him to expect you," said William. "It's quiet up at Laxfirth and visitors are welcome."

And he went out and mounted his pony.

(2)

Not long after his meeting with the minister, William was on his way to visit his father at Laxfirth, where two years earlier, James had bought an estate. This had been a dream of his, to buy a property he could administer and where he could eventually retire. It was somewhere he could return to with his sister and the servants and enjoy periods of peace and quiet which were so essential to his mental health. Not that he wasn't strong and in good condition, still taking an active interest in the business, but now that he had William to rely on, he could afford to leave some of the everyday problems to his son. He still kept up a network of correspondence with other merchants down south, and sometimes travelled to see them himself. Now that he too was a landowner, he could exchange news on a more equal footing with the local lairds and enjoy their company.

Visitors to Shetland began to seek him out at Laxfirth and spend days angling on his estate, or passing through on their way to visit the North Islands.

William still lived at the family home in Lerwick, keeping an eye on the store, having charge of the warehouse, managing other property James owned, seeing to the provisioning of the boats, and many other tasks. A trip to Laxfirth was an outing he welcomed in the course of a busy week.

Now he reached the summit of a hillside and looked down to where, far below, the house at Laxfirth nestled beside an inlet of the sea in the distance. He reined in his pony and looked around, drinking in the beauty of the scene and dreaming that one day all he could see would be his. Ever since he had been at Aberdeen he had had aspirations to own land for himself, to be a gentleman, and to have the sense of well being and security he felt it would bring. Being apprenticed in Hull had somewhat shattered that dream, but now that his father had acquired Laxfirth it had been born again, because surely one day his father's property would be his. Big farms were unknown in Shetland, but he would have a farm, as they did in Yorkshire, where they not only had cattle and ponies but oats and barley and rotations of crops. And if he were a landowner he would build roads for Shetland, not just half a mile like Mr Turnbull, but a road from Laxfirth to Scalloway and Lerwick. As his heart filled with such dreams, his pony carefully picked his way down the steep path to the house.

It was a large stone house with a slate roof and a garden fenced in by high walls as protection against the prevailing winds. Within were clumps of trees, unusual in this bleak landscape, but looking very healthy. William led his pony to the stable where horses and varied shades of Shetland pony were housed, and made his way to the stout wooden door of the house. It stood ajar, and William entered the wide entrance hall and found his father sitting writing a letter at a desk in the drawing room. There was a long window that looked out onto the paved garden from the panelled room, where a painting of James' father and engravings of Edinburgh and other Scottish towns hung on the walls.

"William," exclaimed James, jumping at the sound of his step and putting down his quill pen. "I was concentrating so hard I didn't realise you had come. I'm writing a letter to Mr Gifford. I've never had a daughter married before and it's a strange feeling to think she's old enough to set up home on her own account. I suppose Arthur is a very suitable young man, got the right background and so on, he's presentable and the family are well respected, but I can't help thinking that he's not good enough for Margaret. I suppose the trouble is, no one would ever satisfy me."

"I don't think she's in love with Arthur Gifford," said William. "That's what worries me."

"You young people all have your heads stuffed with this nonsense about romantic love," said James tersely. "It's whether she will make him a good wife and he make her a good husband that counts. Romantic love is something that gets knocked out of you once you settle down to married life. When you have a home and children there's no time for romance. Love's another thing. Real love is something that grows when you live together, when you lose a child or have to face difficult times. When you lose a person you love, it's as if the end of the world has come. I don't think I ever got over the death of your mother."

William was amazed at this expression of deep feeling from his father, whom he always thought incapable of talking about the deeper things of life.

"I shall miss Margaret when she goes," added James, in the same tone. "And I suppose the next thing will be that you will want a wife. We shall have to look out for someone for you."

"I hope to find myself a wife," said William pointedly.

"That's not how things are done," rebuked James gently. "Alliances between families are too precious to be left to the winds of chance. But having said that, I shan't be unreasonable. Perhaps it's time you settled down. Think about it."

"Shall we go out in the garden for a while?" suggested William, wanting to change the subject, while enjoying this new intimacy with his father. "There's a lot come up this week and I need your advice."

And soon the two dark figures, one stocky and balding, the other slim and upright, were in earnest conversation in the garden, strolling under the windblown trees.

(3)

When William saw Margaret again on his return to Lerwick, he told her that James had been writing to Mr Gifford.

"The engagement's official, then," he said. "Everyone seems to be talking about it. Mr Turnbull seemed especially interested."

"Well, he'll be taking the ceremony," said Margaret. "And what are people saying?" she asked, blushing slightly.

"They think it's a good match."

"Don't you agree?"

"I want to know how you think. You don't strike me as a young woman desperately in love. You don't even seem to be particularly happy. I expected you to be radiant and looking forward to a new life. I find you resigned. Margaret, you are my only sister, and I want you to be happy."

"But William, Arthur's father's a laird, and he wants to marry me. He can offer me a good home and security, here in Shetland. He's presentable, he's not bad looking, he has many points in his favour. He's kind and he doesn't lose his temper. I know he likes me. You know him quite well. What have you got against him?"

William was at a loss. Then, "Do you love him?" he asked pointedly.

Margaret turned on him a cool and deliberate glance. At that moment she seemed a lot more than a year older than William.

"If you mean, do I feel about him like the heroines of romantic novels, then the answer is no," she replied. "But I find him acceptable, and I think I could learn to feel affection for him. I think I've grown beyond all that sentimental nonsense we read about at school," she added, smiling, sure of herself. "Our teachers used to try to stop our getting hold of those sorts of books. But we read them all the same. No, Arthur's my age and I wouldn't want to marry an older man. And I want a home of my own. Things are changing here, William. Andrew and James will soon be going down to Liverpool for good. I want my own life too."

William was still frowning, and she persisted, "I don't understand," she said. "Would you have me marry a fisherman? Arthur's a gentleman."

With that William had to be satisfied. He reflected that perhaps she could do worse, and that maybe, like his father, no one she chose would be good enough in his eyes for his sister.

(4)

As spring moved into summer and summer into autumn, and gale winds began to blow and the days shortened, preparations went ahead for Margaret's wedding. Arthur came quite frequently to Lerwick on business, and called to see her, and William, who had known him slightly, got to know him better. He was of medium height, rather thin and with fair hair, and he had a sense of humour which William gradually learned to appreciate. In the end he began to accept the fact that Arthur was to be his brother-in-law.

One day in November when James came to Lerwick, he told William that he had received a letter from Angus Maclean in Aberdeen. "He tells me his daughter Eleanor is getting married at Yuletide," he said, totally unaware of the effect this would produce on William. "We shall both have daughters married. He congratulates me on their engagement."

William took a deep breath and said he hoped Eleanor would be happy.

"She's marrying into one of the richest families in Aberdeen," said James. "Angus is ambitious for his children."

Left to himself William tried to picture Eleanor in his mind, but found that he could not. During his visits to Aberdeen he had never had the opportunity of seeing her. She had been in the country, or away in Edinburgh, and he had left a formal note saying how sorry he had been to miss her.

Strange how he had always got it into his head when he was in Aberdeen that one day he would marry her. Well, this was the end of the dream he had once cherished. He found himself thinking about his sister and her attitude to Arthur. She was embarking on a marriage with her eyes open, not clouded by unreliable emotions. None of the young women whose company he had enjoyed could have been said to have been suitable matches. His father seemed to think that it was time he settled down. He would have to look around and come to a decision. But setting aside his youthful dreams to confront the reality of things was painful. Something infinitely precious had passed out of his life, as though the opal colours of the dawn in all their glory had given way to the glaring and pitiless bright light of midday.

(5)

Margaret was the first of the younger generation to marry and was the envy of her Ogilvy girl cousins. One blustery day when William called at Charles Ogilvy's house he found the four eldest girls gathered together in the drawing room. Barbara, only a year younger than William, and Charlotte, a year younger still, were sewing with difficulty in the dim afternoon light, and put down their work when their cousin entered. Neither girl was pretty, and Barbara had the same pronounced nose as her father, but good sense and warm hearts redeemed their plainness. Elizabeth was nineteen, and was reading a book in the corner. She was quiet and retiring, and didn't impress herself on people. They were all fair, but Margaret, now eighteen and with a lively manner, had golden hair which fell in ringlets to her shoulders. She was standing by the window through which could be glimpsed tall grey houses and a patch of the grey sea of Lerwick harbour. Margaret clapped her hands when she saw that the visitor was William. Since childhood William had had a warm relationship with his cousins and he smiled.

"I see you are all busy," he said. "I think I can guess what you are talking about."

"We want to know about the wedding," said Barbara. "Has it all been arranged?"

"Well, you know it's to be at the New Year," said William, at his ease, sitting down next to Barbara. "There'll be plenty to celebrate this year."

"Yes, but your sister Margaret will be leaving us and going to live somewhere else," put in Charlotte. "Everything will change."

"Don't you like change?" asked cousin Margaret, her eyes shining. "I do. It makes life more exciting."

"When we get married we shall all have to go and live somewhere else, perhaps not see each other very often," pursued Barbara.

"But then you will have a husband, and children, and a house of your own," said Margaret with enthusiasm, and William looked up at his young cousin with her animated expression and laughed. He thought to himself that Margaret was no longer a little goose of a girl but had changed, without his noticing it before, into a rather attractive young woman.

"We shall have a lot of other weddings to look forward to," he said. "Uncle Charles will be bankrupt marrying off all his daughters."

"Well, and there will be Andrina," said Elizabeth. "She has already left school. Her head's stuffed with romantic nonsense."

"Just as well Uncle Ian only has sons," said William. "Your brothers will need careers," he added. "Thomas is to become a merchant like his father and when John and Charles grow up Uncle Charles will have a hard time of it settling them in life too."

"There'll be Uncle Thomas' daughter Agnes," went on Charlotte. "And then Jessie. It'll never stop. But I wonder who will be next?"

"What about you?" asked Barbara shyly. "You'll need a wife too."

"Well, with you four lovely young ladies I hardly need look any further," said William laughing. "But I really came to see Uncle Charles on business. I shall have to go."

"Oh", they chorused in disappointment and made him promise to come again soon.

Later that evening when he returned home, William found himself thinking over the light-hearted conversation he had held with his cousins. Supposing he were to marry one of them? He had never thought of them as possible wives before. He knew them too well, they were too ordinary, and he had taken them for granted. Was that what his father had been subtly hinting at? A family alliance, to cement family ties, and prosper the business? Not a love match at all?

At first he rejected the idea out of hand as it conflicted with all his dreams. Then he began to ask himself why it had not occurred to him before? But he could not go to Uncle Charles and tell him he wanted to marry one of his daughters, and draw straws or throw dice as to which one he should choose. He thought about each one of the girls carefully in turn. Barbara was just too plain, and Charlotte too self-effacing to be his wife. No longer under the sway of a strong emotion, William was able to think more clearly. Elizabeth was too serious and Margaret too young. No, it wouldn't be a solution after all.

But a seed had been sown in his mind, and as he went about his daily tasks he began to think, "What sort of a person am I and what sort of wife do I really need?"

(6)

As Christmas approached Margaret worked hard at her trousseau, invitations were sent out and arrangements made. Family and friends who had a long distance to travel would have to be lodged with relations and neighbours. Margaret was kept very busy and oversaw everything with a cheerful optimism. In the absence of a mother she turned to Aunt Grace, a widow of many years, for support and advice. Her Ogilvy cousins sent to Aberdeen for their new dresses, and happily discussed what they would wear. James laid up a store of drinks, tobacco and little luxuries from an unmentioned source. As the days grew shorter still, an air of expectation hung over William's household. Andrew and James were expected home and there was their news to look forward to. The wedding was to be celebrated in Lerwick and Mr Turnbull the minister from Tingwall was to take the service. Christmas celebrations usually meant endless visits of family and friends entertaining one another until the early hours of the morning with drinking, smoking, eating and dancing to the fiddle until everyone was exhausted. The wedding would be a great fête, and a culmination of the festive season.

The wedding day dawned chilly and wet, and Margaret looked pinched and pale in her elaborate white wedding dress, leaning on James' arm as they walked into the kirk. James himself looked proud and happy in his dark coat and breeches and William was similarly dressed with white stockings and dark shoes with buckles. The weather couldn't spoil the joy of the occasion and family and friends, all in their best attire, smiled and greeted each other in the bare little church.

Up until now William had only been an onlooker at weddings he had attended, now he was the bride's brother and soon perhaps, he would be kneeling with his own bride beside him. As Mr Turnbull turned to address the congregation, and begin the service, smiling too because he knew many of the people there, William tried to concentrate on the words. But instead he found himself watching Arthur Gifford, not much older than himself, stern and nervous at Margaret's side. William was now convinced he cared for Margaret. What a serious step he was about to take, in front of all his relations and friends! Would he, William, have the nerve to do the same? It was the finality of it all that appalled him. A partnership for life. And what if you made a mistake?

He did not have long to reflect like this for soon the service was over and everyone poured out in procession into the inclement air, and cheerfully retired to one of James' Lerwick houses. There a vast meal was served, with the help of many borrowed servants, speeches made, toasts drunk and tears shed. As the afternoon wore on, chairs were cleared away and the fiddlers began to play, gay reels and haunting Shetland tunes, songs brought back by fiddlers on the whaling ships, Scottish dances and plaintive Irish reels. The young people were accomplished and tireless dancers, cousins of all ages from Lerwick and Whalsay and beyond, families who mixed with the Hays socially and on business. The youngest children played noisy games, and Aunt Grace sat with James, Charles Ogilvy and his young wife Anne, Thomas Ogilvy and his wife Andrina, and various members of the older generation. Uncle Ian was there, telling endless stories of other weddings, and gossip and family news was exchanged and glasses filled again and again so that they were all so full of good cheer that they hardly noticed when Margaret and Arthur stole quietly away by themselves, leaving the others to enjoy the rest of the party. James and Andrew who had stayed for the New Year also slipped away as they were setting off south by ship to England the next day.

William laughed and bantered with other young men of his age, and then danced all evening, including, to their great delight, with his Ogilvy girl cousins. When he finally returned home, in the early hours of the morning, drunk with fatigue, he was too tired to reflect that now everything had changed, and that his sister and two brothers had left home for good. He was truly the head of the family.

(7)

One day the following spring, Elizabeth and Margaret Ogilvy went to spend some days at Laxfirth with James Hay and Aunt Grace. Charles Ogilvy's young wife had recently lost a child and was feeling the burden of having taken on such a large young family, especially five grown girls who fiercely resented her usurping their mother in their father's affections. Charles had taken the initiative when matters grew rather tense at home, and asked his cousin if they could come to him for a break where perhaps the change of air would do them good.

William rode over one morning to see his father, and saw them wave from the gate as his pony descended the steep path to the house. Away from their usual surroundings it was easier to consider them not as flighty young girls but as personable young ladies. He walked with them in the garden, shared a meal with them, and suddenly began to realise that he was in fact enjoying himself very much. Both girls obviously enjoyed his company, but he felt more drawn to Margaret, who with her infectious humour usually made him laugh.

But today she seemed very subdued. When Elizabeth had left the room and James had retired he took the opportunity to talk to her alone. He began asking her about her life in Lerwick, and the subject turned to her father and her new stepmother. To his utter consternation, Margaret suddenly held her face in her hands and began to sob uncontrollably.

"Why Margaret, what's the matter?" he asked concerned.

"It's Anne," said Margaret, shaking all over. "She hates me. And I hate her. I hate living at home."

"Margaret." He knelt down beside her and gently placed his arm round her shoulder. "I had no idea you were so unhappy. Does your father know?"

Margaret shook her head.

"He loves her. And he has no time for us any more. Elizabeth doesn't seem to mind. But I miss my mother so much. Whatever shall I do?"

William thought back to that blank loneliness that had overcome him as a child of four when his own mother had died, and thought he understood. He suddenly wanted to sweep Margaret up in his arms in a movement of love and compassion. Impulsively he bent his head and kissed her. Startled, she placed her hands on his shoulders and looked into his face. Then she kissed him too. Taking a deep breath she raised her head and asked him," William, do you love me?"

William felt he was being swept away on a course of action over which he had no control. Instead of answering her directly he put the question to Margaret.

"Do you love me?" he asked.

"I have always loved you William," she said simply. "Ever since I can remember."

"Then will you marry me and come and live with me?"

Events seemed to have overtaken Margaret too. She freed himself from his embrace and smiled through her tears.

"We must think," she said firmly. "We must ask Father."

"I think I know what he will say," said William, his heart beating rather fast, but with a feeling that something crucial had happened. Only he didn't experience a sense of panic but a new kind of happiness deep down inside.

He was even surer when he saw the expression on James' face when he and Margaret went to find him.

"William, this makes me very happy," he said, turning to Margaret and taking both her hands slowly in his and drawing her close to him for a kiss on both cheeks. "Margaret, your father and I have dreamed of this day."

"I must go and tell Elizabeth," said Margaret, suddenly shy. She danced off to find her sister and impart her good news.

(8)

The following months were some of the happiest William ever remembered. He and Margaret were fortunate in having plenty of opportunities to see each other and to get to know one another better. Margaret's sisters, particularly Barbara, were secretly envious of Margaret for being the object of William's choice, but being good-natured girls they were happy for their sister and began to rejoice that he would be an even closer member of the family than before. As William got to know Margaret better and recognised not only her sense of humour and optimism, but also her courage and strength, he began to realise that he had made the right choice.

It was arranged that they should marry before the summer was over and soon there was another joyful celebration and the fiddling and the dancing went on all night because the sun never set.

Shortly after their wedding the couple travelled down to Scotland to stay with friends of James' in Edinburgh.

When they returned, they settled into a house of their own in Lerwick, and before long Margaret had given birth to their first child, a son, whom they christened James, after his grandfather.

CHAPTER FIVE

Inheritance

Some two years later on a bright breezy day early in spring William went up to the harbour at Freefield just north of Lerwick, where James had already built a wide quay and was planning to build more. Freefield was beyond the Fort and the harbour was if anything even safer than in the town. A message had reached William that his father had just arrived in a new ship he had acquired while down on a visit to Edinburgh, and he had sailed up with it on its first journey to Shetland from Leith. Business was going very well and William suspected that his father had some new scheme in mind. They had discussed acquiring a new boat to use for the cod-fishing and William was anxious to see if his father had brought a bargain. James was now over sixty and had always been a gambler by instinct. William found he sometimes had to restrain his father's more wild ideas but James still took considerable responsibility for the business.

The sea was a deep blue and the waves just flecked with white. Several small sailing boats and a cutter were hove to in the harbour, their masts silhouetted against the low yellow-green island of Bressay. Seagulls were wheeling to and fro in the wind and soaring past on the air currents.

As he reached Freefield and strode down to the quay William could see several boats moored there. The first was a small vessel, rigged fore and aft and with one tall mast. The furled sails looked almost new and as he approached he could read her name, *Catherine*. A couple of men were busy on deck and at that moment James came up from the cabin, his sparse hair blown wild by the wind.

"Well, what do you think of her?" was his first question. Father and son both shared a love of boats and soon they were reviewing all her qualities from the fixed bowsprit to the finish of the deck and the interior fittings.

"I'm planning to go out with her to the cod-fishing," said James with enthusiasm. "This little ship will be ideal. We can use her for trading trips round the islands, and for further afield as well."

"Otherwise you had a good trip to Edinburgh?" asked William.

"Well, yes, and I have another surprise in store for you. I've acquired another ship, called the *George Rose*, and she'll be coming up in a few days. I want to use her for herring fishing. You know it's been my dream to develop the herring fishing here."

William was aware that his father had always felt it was unfair that the herring fishing should be left to the Dutch. Each June their fleet congregated in Bressay Sound and Lerwick was invaded by skippers and seamen in their dark blue jerseys and baggy trousers, smoking pipes and talking Dutch. One of their chief forms of entertainment was to hire Shetland ponies and ride out into the hills, or try out their English on the woman knitters who walked into town to sell their wares. Before William was born James had given evidence to a Parliamentary Commission about the suitability of developing herring fishing in Shetland, but in the end nothing had come of it. James himself had made several other attempts to set up herring fishing with a company from Yarmouth, but to no avail. Hostility on the part of local lairds also engaged in fishing had brought these schemes to nought.

"This time I've arranged to have a dozen Dutch fishermen sent over to teach our men how to fish for herring," continued James. "And with this new boat especially fitted out, surely we can't go wrong? With all their knowledge of the sea, our Shetlanders must be able to fish for herring themselves. It just needs someone to organise it on a commercial scale."

James arranged for his goods to be sent on into Lerwick and agreed to walk back with William. His son was surprised at his sprightliness and good humour. He took him back to see Margaret and the children and to continue talking about his journey.

The *Catherine* was duly fitted out and put into service for the cod-fishing and set out on her first trip. When the *George Rose* arrived, she was inspected and deemed to be ideal for the task in hand. But the herring fishing was not a success, and William watched his father sink into one of his frequent depressions and moodiness. He retired to Laxfirth, where gradually the peace and beauty and isolation prevailed, and he recovered, only to begin dreaming again.

(2)

William Hay had lived most of his life in the shadow of the European War, first the aftermath of the French Revolution and Napoleon's meteoric rise to power, and then his victories in Europe, news of which reached Lerwick via the frequent contacts with navy ships, and trading vessels which called there. Dutch fishermen brought horrific tales of the destruction of their homes in Holland and trading routes to Norway were cut off by the war. James could no longer send fish to Spain and for a number of years the British blockade of shipping had even restricted opportunities for smuggling.

The news of Napoleon's abdication at Fontainebleau in April 1814 and his exile to the island of Elba soon reached Lerwick.

One evening in May Mr Barry and Mr McCulloch, two veteran officers from the Fort, were enjoying William's hospitality at home. They dined on fish, chicken, lamb, beef, puddings, tarts, cabbage, pea soup and beans. James had joined them, and when they were left alone, they began discussing the peace.

"Twenty-two years of war, and now it's over," said Mr McCulloch. "It's hard to realise we have peace again."

"I was only six when the war began," said William, pouring them drinks of brandy. "I hardly know what peace is like."

"They had fireworks in Edinburgh," said Mr Barry. "But it was a bit of a shock to find we were being sent up to Lerwick."

"Do you think they will keep a garrison in the Fort?" asked James.

"It's early days yet," said Mr McCulloch. "You are on the northward route to the West Indies, and that's important."

"Where did you serve?" asked William, always interested to hear of other people's experiences.

"I've been to Malta," replied Mr McCulloch, "and I was at the battle of the Nile."

"Then you've seen the Pyramids and the Sphinx?"

"I have and they're a grand sight," said Mr McCulloch. "One of the wonders of the world."

"I've been in Spain," said Mr Barry. "Spain's a wild country. Some of the women are dark looking, like North Africans. But it's not easy to get to know them."

"I went to Spain before the war," said James, reminiscing. "Barcelona and Malaga. A very colourful place."

"Lerwick looks quite attractive from the harbour," said Mr Barry, changing the subject. "But you can't see it properly because of all the warehouses."

"Lodberries we call them," said William.

"But once you come ashore the stink of fish rather sickens you," said Mr McCulloch. "And it's not much bigger than a village."

"As we came up in the ship last week, there was a thick mist," began Mr Barry. "I was up on deck and suddenly a boat pulled astern of the ship out of the fog without any warning, and then disappeared just as quickly out of sight. There were about six men dressed in skin coats and breeches, with long hip boots on their legs, and they had long fair hair to their shoulders, and woollen caps on their heads."

"Those were our Shetland fishermen," said William. "The boats are called sixerns, they carry six men, and they go out to the deep-sea fishing for ling and cod, they call it the haaf fishing up here."

"They go out of sight of land in those little boats?" asked Mr McCulloch amazed.

"They might go thirty miles," said William. "All they take with them apart from their lines is oatmeal and water to make porridge."

"Fishing is the mainstay of these islands, all our men are fishermen," explained James. "The women stay at home and look after the crofts and the animals."

"And what do they catch?"

"Cod mainly, and ling. There are the herring fishing grounds, but that's still mostly the preserve of the Dutch. We have made some moves to try to establish herring fishing for ourselves."

"Where I come from on the north coast of Scotland they fish for herring from small boats," said Mr Barry.

"They do in Orkney," said James. "We commissioned a large boat for herring. I think perhaps we were on the wrong tack. We'll win in the end."

"Where do you export the fish?" enquired Mr McCulloch.

"We've been exporting to Dublin and Belfast, and to Liverpool," said William. "And we've started buying up cattle and ponies from local sales and sending them south."

"You have your own boats?" asked Mr Barry.

"We have a number of small boats for the fishing trade, they go up the coast to collect the dried fish," explained William. "We've just acquired two bigger ships, capable of going off to Spain or Norway."

James and William went on to explain about the store in Lerwick and how they had licences to sell tea and coffee. They told them at length how they found crews for the whaling ships going to Greenland, and provided stores for them.

William told them that he was an agent for the Commercial Bank in Shetland.

"It's a risky business financing the fishing trade," he said. "You are not only pitting your wits against the market, and against storms and bad weather. You are gambling on having a good fishing season every year, and it doesn't always happen."

"We've had a very good evening Mr Hay. But we mustn't outstay our welcome."

"I hope you will come again," said William courteously, with a little bow. "We are always pleased to see visitors. And just as sad to see them go," he added. "We're a very close-knit society here in Shetland."

"I shall be delighted to see either of you up at Laxfirth," added James. " I have a property in Tingwall. You are very welcome to come there for some fishing."

The two officers formally took their leave, and went off praising the hospitality of the Shetlanders they had met, here in this barren northern land to which they felt they had been exiled.

(3)

The last time James had returned from Edinburgh he had been to see a lawyer. He had mentioned to William that he had the intention of visiting Mr Allen, but had not told him why. When he returned he called on his son carrying a fat parcel out of which he produced a large parchment.

"William," he said solemnly, and there was something in the tone of his voice that made William realise this was no ordinary occasion. "I'm getting on in years, and the day may come when I shall no longer be here."

"Father," protested William.

"And I've decided," went on James, "that the time has come for me to pass on to you all my property. I don't want it to wait till my death. It's all in this document – the property in Lerwick, in Yell, in Whalsay, the land I bought in Northmavine for the fishing, all the ships, the store, warehouse, and the rest of the business. It's all yours."

William took a deep breath. Just as it was a momentous step for James to renounce his inheritance and pass it on to his son, so for William it was a very special moment when he realised that he had come into a considerable fortune.

"I have Laxfirth," said James. "The rest is yours. For you to do as you wish."

William paused for a moment. Not long ago his father-in-law Charles Ogilvy had bought an estate outside Lerwick called Seafield. William had been there often and was impressed by the solid built mansion with its fine staircase, the garden and surrounding fields Charles planned to turn into a farm. It was the property of a successful merchant. William dreamed of doing the same.

"I want to buy a property outside Lerwick. Where I can raise my family, and run a farm. Like Charles Ogilvy."

James looked hard at his son.

"You'd be a fool," he said sharply. "You are too ambitious."

"But I shan't take away with one hand what I've given with the other. What you do with your inheritance is your affair. I suppose we all have our dreams."

Only when William had time by himself to examine the document did be begin to understand the extent of the fortune he now possessed. He was not only a joint partner in a successful business. He was now the owner of considerable property. Although he had had greater responsibility of recent years, he had always felt that final decisions rested with his father. Now James had stepped down and he was the person in charge. It was a heady and somewhat daunting thought. It was as if at long last he had really come of age.

(4)

Later in May James set out in the sloop *Catherine* to go to the cod-fishing southwest of Foula. He seemed rather excited about something as routine as a fishing expedition, and was secretive when William asked him about it. William thought it was an unwise plan but if James had abdicated from his position as head of the business, he was still as obstinate as ever, and nothing would make him change his mind. William wondered secretly whether his father perhaps regretted handing everything over and needed to think he was still involved.

He was gone for over two months.

One afternoon in July, William returned home to find the Customs Officer waiting at his house. He was someone William knew well and he greeted him in a friendly manner. But the officer's expression was stern and he did not return William"s greeting.

"I'm here on business," he said briefly, at once banishing any room for camaraderie. "When were you last in contact with your father Mr James Hay?"

William's heart sank. He had learned as a young boy not to say too much about his father's whereabouts when he was probably engaged in illegal activities, and the possibility that James was still now involved in smuggling suddenly crossed his mind. He resolved to say as little as possible, but all the same felt relieved that he could with honesty tell him nothing.

"My father set off in May for Foula for the cod-fishing," he said. "Since then we have had no news."

"Come now, Mr Hay, " said the officer impatiently. "You know very well that one of your boats was searched in Leith earlier this year on suspicion of carrying smuggled goods."

"She was released without charge," said William quickly. "Because there was nothing to find."

"Mr Hay, we know that your father has been involved in smuggling for years," continued the officer, renewing his attack. "Only he's had the good fortune up till now not to get caught in the act."

"What are you telling me?" asked William.

"Your ship the *Catherine* has been seized on its way to Orkney with your father James Hay on board. She has been taken into Kirkwall and impounded on suspicion of smuggling. Now will you tell me what you know?"

"I swear I know nothing," reiterated William. "He bought the *Catherine* for cod-fishing and perhaps for trips up the coast to the North Isles." He paused, unsure just what the authorities knew. "But I am most glad to know that he is safe."

"Illegal trade has increased since the peace," said the officer. "It's got to be stamped out. And with all due respect Mr Hay, prominent people like your father should set an example. If he is charged and found guilty, he'll be severely punished and then the lesser fry will surely think twice before trying it again."

"I have no knowledge of this affair whatsoever," said William firmly. "You know full well I have never been guilty of smuggling. Please convey to the authorities that I am anxious to see my father home as soon as possible. I'm afraid I have nothing more to say."

The officer seemed to sense that William was either unwilling or unable to incriminate his father, and that further questions would be fruitless. With a curt little bow he turned and took his leave. William remained with his heart full of conflicting emotions, furious that his father should have put him in such an uncompromising position, but at the same time intensely desirous to know the truth of the matter.

Eventually James arrived back at William's house in Lerwick, on a rainy day, bedraggled and totally dispirited.

William had foreseen a stormy session with his father, but the older man did not seem to be in a mood to fight.

"Well," he said, sitting down heavily at the table and putting his head in his hands. "They released me without charge. They said they suspected but couldn't prove anything. But they reckon my fortune was made through smuggling, and that's not true."

"Not entirely true," he corrected himself. "But I have been a smuggler and now I've been caught." He looked at William, whose feelings of exasperation and then pity changed to compassion as he listened to his father. "William, I wanted you to be proud of me. Now you will despise me."

William ignored this remark and said with concern, "Father, anything could have happened to you. You could have disappeared in a storm. How should I have felt if they had brought me news that you were dead? Where on earth have you been?"

"Well, we did go to Foula for the cod-fishing but we didn't catch much. So first we went down to Orkney to Sanday where I negotiated with some of the local farmers for a cargo of meal and potatoes for Norway."

"But it's illegal to export grain," said William quickly. "You know that. And it's forbidden to go to Norway."

"Yes," said James a little shamefacedly. "Anyway we went to Bergen. I saw Captain Peterson and some of his friends. It was the first time we had seen each other for years and it was worth the risk. He got me a cargo of hides for London."

"And what did you do in London?" asked William, impatient to hear the end of the story.

"I loaded cordage for Hull," said James. "But instead of Hull we went to Rotterdam for Dutch gin and came up here to Shetland. We were off-loading casks of gin on the west coast for a couple of nights."

"And I had no idea you were here," said William. "Just as well, or the officer would have known I was lying. Father, why did you do it?"

A glint of light came into James' weary eyes. "I suppose it's like the gambling instinct," he said. "You always think you can win. And a smuggler always thinks he can get away with it. It wasn't for the money. It was for the excitement of taking a risk of proving that you can still do it."

As he relived his trip James seemed transformed. William suddenly realised with exasperation that it wasn't a question of morality for him, but an absorbing game of outwitting the Excise men.

"Well, then we went back to Orkney and negotiated another cargo of grain before we took the rope from London into Kirkwall. But someone from the Customs in Shetland had seen a small boat lying at anchor off Sumburgh Head, and when they investigated they found not only eels but also casks of Dutch gin. The only ship that had been in the vicinity was the *Catherine*. They went on ahead of us and we were escorted into Kirkwall."

"But they didn't prosecute you," said William, surprised.

"I shall never know why," said James.

"You had this planned for ages," said William, with sudden insight. "Haven't you? Even when you brought the *Catherine* up from Leith for the first time?"

"It had crossed my mind that she would be a useful ship for smuggling," conceded James meekly.

"And you weren't even fined?" pursued William.

"My property is yours now," said James. "They couldn't touch it."

He suddenly looked a very old man.

Later that evening when James had left and William was still pondering over his father's exploits, he suddenly realised that even the timing of the transfer of the property had all been part of the plan too.

But it was James' last smuggling venture. From now on he seemed a beaten man, and he returned to Laxfirth, concentrating on developing his estate and keeping up with old acquaintances.

(5)

When the real peace came after the battle of Waterloo and the Navy stopped sending press-gangs to impress Shetlanders, William already had three children. The following year he bought a large house and several fields outside Lerwick, which he named Hayfield. It had three stories and a wide and imposing staircase up to the front door, and he felt it suited his success as a merchant and his status in Lerwick society. Roundabout, the scattalds or commons where the ordinary people grazed their cattle and sheep, had been enclosed as fields. It was only a short ride across and down the windy lanes to Lerwick harbour, or over to the new quays at Freefield. There were more merchants than ever trading from Lerwick, more lodberries built out into Bressay Sound and the town was growing.

In 1819 William's brother Andrew, whose merchant venture in Liverpool had not met with success, joined the East India Company and went out to Calcutta. From there he soon moved on to the island of Singapore, then a new colony only just founded by Sir Stamford Raffles. In his letters Andrew wrote enthusiastically of trading possibilities in the developing port, the hot and humid climate, the surrounding jungle, the exciting unfamiliar Asiatic world, where most of the local population were Chinese or Malay. There were still very few Europeans though the new town was being laid out and fortified. Andrew was obviously fascinated by all he saw and was enjoying himself. William, whose own career was very fulfilling, did not envy his brother, but he secretly thought that it was perhaps just as well they were far enough apart not to intrude on each others' lives and to preclude rivalry or jealousy.

CHAPTER SIX

Prosperity

One day five years later William was with his father-in-law Charles Ogilvy at Freefield, inspecting a herring boat in the process of being built with timber from Norway. Charles' two sons, Charles and John, now twenty, had joined him in his business, and William saw a lot of them. They often called at Hayfield to drink tea or coffee and discuss business. Charles senior was now rather bent and his hair was white. William, still lithe and dark, towered above him as they stood in the cold east wind that was whipping up waves over the harbour in spite of the sun trying to come through the clouds. There was a sharp odour of tar and sawdust in the air and their conversation was punctuated by the banging of the carpenters' hammers.

"These half-decked boats are such an improvement on our open sixerns," said William. "The fishermen have got that much more protection."

"Ay, I think they are safer," agreed Charles.

"To think that the herring fishery is really taking off up here," said William with enthusiasm. "There have been so many attempts up till now and they have all failed."

"Everything's expanding," said Charles, pulling up his collar against the wind. "Are you still thinking of having a dock built here?"

"I've thought about a dock here in Shetland ever since I was in Hull," said William. "Somewhere boats could be repaired and shipping lie low for the winter."

"Retail sales are growing fast too," said Charles. "Do you realise we had over sixty whaling ships here in Lerwick last year?"

"Yes, but as the value of sales increases, we have to import more and more money to fit out the sailors going to Greenland," said William. "What we need is our own bank. Being agent for the Commercial Bank isn't enough."

"Come back with me," said Charles suddenly. "There's something I've been meaning to ask you for some time. I want you to think it over and let me know your decision. You don't have to make up your mind straightaway."

William's curiosity was aroused as they turned back into the cold wind and began walking in the direction of the Fort. Ahead of them rose the cliff and across the water the low sun cast long shadows from the boats into the sea.

"We've agreed business is going well," began Charles. "You've proved yourself as a successful merchant and you're striking out on your own. My future's assured now that Charles and John both seem to have a head for business. What would you say if we went into partnership?"

William's first reaction was surprise. It had not occurred to him that his father-in-law would flatter him with such an offer. Thinking quickly he could see that together they would control quite a wide area of local business. It would bring them even closer together.

"You've got a lot of forward-looking ideas," went on Charles, as William did not reply. "We should complement each other. You've built up a lot of useful contacts that could help us both."

In his mind William saw the piles of letters back in his counting-house that came regularly from all the business centres of England as well as firms in Edinburgh, Glasgow, Perth, Dundee and Aberdeen. In some places he already had a number of correspondents, some of them inherited from his father, and others he dealt with he had discovered through personal visits or mutual acquaintances. He had learnt a good deal of discretion since he was in Hull and did not immediately respond to Charles' proposal. However Charles suggested they each assess every aspect of the business they did so that they could see what a partnership would involve.

When they reached Lerwick's main street they parted on friendly terms and William made his way back to Hayfield with a host of things to think over.

(2)

Business in Shetland was booming because expectations were high and the economy was expanding. William had more opportunities to put his own creative ideas into practice now that his father had retired and the main responsibility for the business was his. But James was still respected locally in spite of the episode of the *Catherine*, which was now common knowledge, and many merchants tended to attribute William's prosperity to the business experience of his father. It is always hard for a son or a daughter to shine when they remain in the same sphere as a successful parent and William had had to prove himself in his own right. His father was a charismatic sort of character who immediately attracted attention, but little by little William had established himself as a person to be reckoned with, even if his successes were firmly built on the foundations James had laid.

His first venture had been in the area of cod fishing. Traditionally the lairds had controlled their tenants' fishing, making it a compulsory part of their rents, and forcing them to buy goods at their own stores, often reducing them to a state of servitude from which they had no escape. William too wanted to set up fishing stations, where local men could share in the ownership of a boat and bring in cod to be cured and dispatched by his company. He had begun by buying the tack of the lands in Oxna, and looking out for more land to purchase.

To transport the salted fish more and more small boats would be needed for the coastal trade and William had great plans to expand the harbour facilities at Freefield and build his own boats for both cod and herring fishing.

Another of James' dreams had been realised with the founding of the Zetland Herring Company. William and Charles Ogilvy had been among the first subscribers. Small half-decker boats were built for Shetland in Orkney and men used to herring fishing brought north from Scotland. For the first time Shetlanders began to enjoy a share in the herring fishing.

After all his efforts and success in building up his company, William wondered if it would be wise to go into partnership with someone older and more experienced than he was? Would he still have the final say in important decisions?

That night his wife found him sitting at the table with his head on his hands, staring into the distance.

"Is something worrying you?" she asked, laying her hand gently on his shoulder.

He looked up at her, recollecting himself, and smiled.

"I've got a big decision to make," he said. "Well, it concerns us both. Your father wants us to go into partnership."

"Why William, that would be wonderful," said Margaret enthusiastically, seeing the business as one future happy family.

"Margaret, I'm not so sure. It wasn't easy for me to work closely with my father. I know he is a difficult man and your father is different. But I wouldn't want differences over business to upset our lives."

He did not add that he was secretly determined not to allow himself to be unduly influenced by his father-in-law. If there was to be a partnership, then it had to be a partnership of equals, even if he was the younger man.

"Father's a very fair person," pursued Margaret. "He would never take advantage of you."

"And I should never take advantage of him," said William firmly. But the thought of his father's and Charles Ogilvy's smuggling activities rose to his mind. He would insist that affairs were on a different footing.

"Surely if you are both doing well, you can only do better together?" suggested Margaret.

"It might give us an edge over our rivals," agreed William. And he began to consider the offer from a purely business point of view.

It did not take him long to see the practical advantages of Charles' offer. And so the firm of Hay and Ogilvy's was set up, and a remarkable partnership began. It occurred at a propitious moment, and its success and prosperity mirrored the growth of Shetland's economy. Together the two men planned the expansion of Freefield, with the creation of docks, quays and warehouses and a shipbuilding yard where fishing boats and trading vessels could be built and repaired. Curing stations for fish were established in many parts of Shetland, and soon the firm became a byword for prosperity in the islands.

(3)

A year or two before Charles and William agreed to go into partnership, on a chilly winter's afternoon, members of the Shetland Society had met in a draughty ill-lit room in Lerwick, principally to discuss the viability of setting up a bank in Shetland. William had been one of those invited, together with other merchants and local landowners, all of them soberly dressed and in sombre mood. The room smelt of tobacco smoke and damp leather boots and was so dark they needed tall candelabra on the table to enable the secretary to read the proposals. As the steady hum of conversation died away he stood up and addressed the gathering.

"Gentlemen," he began. "You all know that the chief matter on our agenda today is the proposal put forward by Mr Arthur Nicolson." He indicated a large florid dark-haired man sitting beside him. "Mr Nicholson wants us to discuss the formation of our own Shetland Bank here in Lerwick."

All eyes were on Arthur Nicolson as he rose to his feet and took a deep breath. "Gentlemen and fellow members," he said. "I know that most of you have accounts with bankers in Edinburgh or maybe in Aberdeen. But you must all be only too aware that up here in Shetland ready money is in short supply and a local bank would provide credit to boost our local economy. If we could gain the financial support of local people of means it would be of great advantage to the neighbourhood."

As a few heads began to nod in agreement, he continued, "I suggest we raise twenty thousand pounds and that we issue our own notes. But we need backers and if we don't get them the scheme will come to nothing. What do you think?"

One of those present was a small, dark, astute-looking man, one of the island's most influential lairds, William Mouat. His estate was one of the largest in Shetland and his support would be crucial to launch the bank.

"Twenty thousand pounds is a lot of money," he said cautiously. "The life of these islands depends on fishing as much as on agriculture. And if you can't count on the harvest, neither can you rely on the fishing. It's hardly like investing in a textile mill or a foundry."

William Hay, one of the youngest present, was intensely interested in the debate. Ever since he had been established at Hayfield he had been an agent for the Commercial Bank, and the idea of having a bank in Shetland was another of the dreams he had brought back with him from Hull.

"One of the biggest problems of fishing in these islands is that to prosper the fishermen need money in advance, they need credit to pay for their boats, their lines and so on."

His earnestness seemed to irritate William Mouat who went a little red and interposed firmly," But Mr Hay, we're not in the business of setting up a bank for fishermen."

"No, but we merchants need money to supply the men and their families," said William, standing his ground.

"And the whalers," said another member of the group.

"Mr Mouat, prosperity depends on having a supply of credit," said a tall solemn man sitting at the back. He was another merchant and a friend of Charles Ogilvy's. "Commerce means being ready to take a risk and to reap a reward you have to risk money in advance. A local bank is just what we need at present."

But it was one thing to put forward ambitious plans and quite another to persuade enough people of influence to join the scheme and provide the financial backing that would make it work. Lending money was a risk for, with no limited liability, a lender risked all his fortune if the bank failed. In the end, to William's disappointment, not enough of those present could finally be persuaded to give the bank their support, a vote was taken and the motion was defeated.

Later William discussed the matter with Charles Ogilvy, and in due course they came up with a scheme of their own to launch a Shetland Bank, on a much smaller scale than originally planned, mainly to finance their own trading business and fishing concerns. In the heady moments of their new partnership and at the height of their success the risk did not seem to be too great, and both of them were equally persuaded that it was just what Shetland needed. It did not occur to either of them to keep the accounts of Hay and Ogilvy and the Shetland Bank separate, and they soon found themselves granting each other loans for personal investments in property and expenses. William, who had already bought large acres of land in the Tingwall Valley to expand the Laxfirth estate, spent a great deal of money buying property for himself and his family, and establishing himself as an important Shetland landowner. It all went hand in hand with the expansion of the business

(4)

A year or two after they had agreed to go into partnership, William sat at home one day inspecting the plans drawn up for the new dock at Freefield. He was very keen on this project and was determined it should be a success. With knit brow he made several notes along the side of the big plan in front of him and then stood up and pushed it away as the younger Charles Ogilvy was shown into the room.

"What's the haste?" asked William, as Charles sat down panting. His long fair hair was ruffled and his blue eyes anxious.

"Do you know that John Mouat has plans to build his own dock at Garthspool?" he blurted out. "Surely it will take away half our business?"

Garthspool was a little further out from Freefield along to the north of the bay, but enjoying equally fine conditions for a harbour. Traditionally the fish trade had been in the hands of the lairds, the local landowners who controlled the life of the area. Now though, merchants like William Hay were taking over much of the business and through their wealth beginning to rival them in influence. William came of a family of ministers and merchants who mixed easily with the higher ranks of society, yet there were one or two of the lairds who resented the way he had bought land and was acquiring power and prestige. One man in particular, William Mouat, seemed to object to William's new position and never became a friend. He was hostile to any suggestions that William put forward in the Shetland Society, and this in spite of the fact that William and William Mouat's son John had collaborated quite successfully in business in the past. However William Hay was always of the opinion that John had got where he was less through his own drive and ability but thanks to his father's pedigree and position in life. And now it looked as if the Mouats were about to steal a march on Hay and Ogilvy's. They would have to launch a counter-offensive.

William's reaction was not as impulsive as Charles'. He had never made a secret of his scheme, nor had he really ever imagined that his would be the only dock in Shetland.

"Come Charles, it's a bit of a blow, but it's not the end of the world," he said encouragingly. "One thing's for sure, I bet it wasn't his own idea. His father will have put him up to it. I expect you are right, he's doing it to compete with us. No one else round here is in a position to challenge us."

"So what shall we do?"

William thought rapidly. He had been enjoying a quiet moment by himself congratulating himself on the excellence of his design. Now that luxury had been destroyed but he didn't intend to let the initiative pass to John Mouat. He stroked his chin and said in measured tones, "Well, I think we'll have to push forward the building of the dock, and I'll consult with your father to see if we can't employ more men. If ours is the first to be completed, then we shall get the first clients."

"We can keep an eye on Garthspool to see how it's getting on," said Charles eagerly.

"I'll come round to see your father in the morning," said William. "In any case I intended to show him the revision I've made to the plans. But now it all seems more urgent than we thought. Take the plan round with you now, and he can see just what's involved."

After Charles had left William sighed. Apart from his father, William quite liked John Mouat. He was an affable, easy-going fellow and not the sort of person he would really want to hurt. But if business were to prosper, he could not allow any rival, even if they had done him favours in the past, to get ahead of him. So he sat there racking his brains for a way to win through. But no ideas came and he ruefully put away his things and went to find his family.

Next day at Charles Ogilvy's house, both sons, John and Charles, were there to greet him. Both tall, fair-haired and blue-eyed with their father's large nose and jaw; it was easy to see that they were brothers.

"This puts us in a bit of a spot," said Charles senior. "Even if we take on more men the work won't get finished this year."

"That's what I'm afraid of," said William. "We shall lose any advantage. At present I can't see any answer."

"Father, I've been thinking," said John suddenly. "Surely the parish boundary runs down just the other side of Freefield? So Garthspool is well outside the town. Won't John Mouat have to pay customs duties on all goods he brings into Lerwick?"

"My God, you've hit on it," said William, banging his hand on the table. "That's it. Any goods outside Lerwick have to pay duty. I don't suppose John Mouat thought of that."

"Well, nor did we," said the younger Charles wryly. "What can we do about it?"

"We shall have to go carefully," said Charles senior. "Some of the people in town are convinced that we use Freefield for smuggling in any case. Still more Garthspool. They can't see why we shouldn't pay taxes on our goods too."

"I think I'll go and see the Collector of Customs," said William getting up. "Perhaps I can talk him round to our way of thinking. The Mouats aren't the only people round here with influence."

In due course the docks were built, but William and Charles Ogilvy won the day, and John Mouat did initially have to suffer a handicap by having to pay extra dues on his goods. However, business was so brisk that at the time both firms prospered.

(5)

One fine day William rode up to Veensgarth in the Tingwall Valley with David Nicolson, a fellow merchant from Lerwick. They had gone up to inspect the property that William had bought, one of the estates he had acquired in the area. They reined in their horses near some tumbledown crofts and surveyed the green and pleasant landscape. This land was fertile and somewhat sheltered and a few stunted thorn bushes had managed to survive the onslaughts of the winter winds.

William had just come back from a trip down south to Leith in the schooner *Norna*.

"We had a rough trip," he began, as they gazed around them. "It was stormy nearly all the way from Lerwick. They reefed every sail, brought down every inch of canvas and we took in a lot of water. Then the gale decreased to a strong breeze. It took us two days and two nights what with the weather and calling in at all the little harbours down the Scottish coast. On the way back the weather had changed. It was fine and there was almost no wind. Then when a breeze did get up, the high tide had passed and we had to wait till next day to sail. Consequently I have only just got back."

David Nicolson was about ten years younger than William. He was tall and dark with an intelligent face. They had known each other for a long time. David had a great respect for William as a merchant and valued his friendship.

"Did you stay in Edinburgh?" he asked.

"My friends have a house near Charlotte Square," said William. "And James is now in Edinburgh in school. On this visit I had a chance to visit the Highland Agricultural Society and see all their latest ideas in agriculture. It's amazing all the things they've got on show: ploughs and drills and all sorts of equipment. But what interested me most are their ideas on breeding cattle and sheep. Some farmers have vastly improved their stock by selective breeding. I should like to turn Veensgarth into a farm where I can rear fine cattle to send down south. Horses too."

"Yes, and I know they are experimenting with rotations of crops, new strains, clover and turnips," put in David.

"Yes, and turnips are not just good for the soil," said William. "It's no longer necessary to kill off all our cattle in winter."

"What a business that was!" said David. "Slaughtering cattle down by the lodberries. As bloody as a whale kill."

"Down south they're enclosing the common lands," continued David. "Even turning people off their own land to make room for sheep. Up here the sheep run wild up the hills."

"Down south it's the landowners who are making their land productive," insisted William. "They're the people who are investing in the mills and factories and making the economy boom. Industry's thriving because of the success of agriculture."

"These islands can't compete with the mainland," said David wistfully. "Our resources are too few, our land too poor."

"Nevertheless I am determined to get a successful farm started here," said William. "As a boy I always dreamed of becoming a landowner, of looking round me and having the satisfaction of knowing that all I could see belonged to me. Now I have actually achieved it, I can see that I've got responsibilities too, to improve the land and make it productive."

"Shall we ride on to Laxfirth," he continued, "and see what new-fangled ideas my father has introduced since I've been away?"

(6)

Days when he was aware of his own happiness, such as that sunny morning down at Veensgarth, with a friend for company, the beauty of the summer landscape, and dreams of the future to spur him on, were rare, because happiness is mostly seen in retrospect. Yet all through his thirties fortune seemed to smile on William, bringing him success and prosperity in every area of life. He had a happy relationship with his wife Margaret, who had brought him eleven children, of whom only two had died. Unlike his sister Margaret's marriage. They had not been able to have children, and frustration and disappointment had brought Margaret to a depression not unlike her father's, and Arthur to drink heavily. For William and Margaret their worst moment had come when their beloved two-year-old daughter Janet had died suddenly of a fever. Margaret had been distraught, and the only thing that had helped William was the thought that he must comfort his wife.

An onlooker might have reasoned that perhaps the gods had sent them this misfortune to prevent them becoming too proud, for in everything else William seemed the envy of his contemporaries. He was now a rich landowner, his estate among the ten foremost in Shetland. By the time he was forty, Hay and Ogilvy's had established fishing stations all over Shetland, and had a fleet of ships that took the salted fish as far as Spain and the West Indies. They owned over a hundred fishing boats, and supplied men with lines and equipment. They had developed a deepwater quay at Scalloway from which fishing crews could fish for cod. William's retail store, which had also finally merged with Hay and Ogilvy's, was doing a good trade, and James, William's younger brother, who had now gone out to work for a timber firm in New Brunswick, sent over consignments of timber.

Charles Ogilvy had been appointed vice-consul for Denmark and was well-known by all the visitors who came to the islands. William too was at the height of his powers and was accepted as part of the best local society. He irradiated self-confidence and well-being, and for a while it seemed that nothing could shake him.

(7)

At forty William's hair began to tinge with grey. But Charles Ogilvy was old and bent, and during that year he handed over control of his business to his sons Charles and John and retired to Seafield.

One afternoon that summer on a perfect day when the sun shone in a bright blue sky and the air was comfortably warm, William and Margaret and their family were sitting out in the walled garden they had had built at Hayfield. Here, sheltered from the prevailing winds, a few sturdy trees and bushes had managed to establish themselves. Clumps of honeysuckle and roses vied with white and yellow daisies, and pink and purple lupins, while there were beds of strawberries that would soon be ripe. It was a rare day of rest for William and as he sat on a cane chair and shielded his eyes from the sun, he looked around at his assembled family with pride.

James, now sixteen, was home from school. He was a dark, handsome and intelligent boy, the apple of his father's eye. William had great plans for James, who would grow up to inherit his father's wealth and position. Next to him on the grass were Charles and William, both born in the same year and at school in Edinburgh too. Andrew was a chubby fair boy of nine, Laurence a pale thin child of five, John Ogilvy a toddler of three with fair curly hair and Arthur Gifford a baby in his mother's arms. There were two girls, Barbara, who was thirteen, tall and dark and good-looking like her father, and Anne, eight, shorter and with her mother's golden fair hair.

William looked too at his wife, whose hair had gone white, and whose face was already lined with wrinkles, though she was several years younger than he was. She had been a good wife to him, and supported him in all he did. He had never regretted his marriage; it seemed to have brought him all he wanted.

Margaret caught him looking at her and smiled.

"It's one of those days we shall remember," she said. "How often do we get a day like this in Shetland?"

A short while later the bell rang and the maid came out with a sealed note.

"It's from Seafield, I think it's important," she whispered to William.

Something gave William a sense of foreboding. He opened the letter and scanned it quickly.

"Bad news?" asked Margaret, watching the smile drain from his face.

"It's your father," he said dully. "He's dead."

It was not only a sad end to a lovely afternoon. It was the end of a long partnership, a long friendship with a man he had known all his life, a man he loved and trusted. A man who was also his father-in-law and grandfather to his children.

"Uncle Charles has died," he said to the children who had sensed something awful had happened. "Come Margaret, it had to happen one day," he said to his wife, and putting his arm round her, led her into the house.

Looking back, he realised it was also the end of a period in life that would never return.

CHAPTER SEVEN

Shadows

Four years later, the end came too for James. He lay on his bed at Laxfirth, his face pale, waxen like a piece of dried parchment, and he breathed heavily. By his side sat William, who had been sent for urgently and who had arrived the evening before. He watched his father in the flickering candlelight, willing himself to stay awake, chastened to see him so helpless, his strength almost gone. But James lived through the early hours of the morning, calling for drinks of water in a steady voice. The spring dawn soon came; filling the stuffy sickroom with light and making the old man look paler and more drawn than ever. Now his breathing was shallow and William gazed at the pale blue veins protruding from his forehead and his gnarled hand lying on the coverlet.

"William."

The voice startled William who was surprised at its strength. His father's eyes had opened and gazed lucidly at him.

"I'm glad you've come. There's a lot I want to say to you but I don't think I have much time left. We've had our ups and downs I know, but I want us to part good friends."

"Father." William's voice choked as he squeezed James' hand.

"You've achieved far more than I did. I've lived to see you a prosperous merchant and I'm proud of you. I hope you live to be as proud of James as I am of you. I hope all your children do as well."

James paused for breath.

"I want you to promise to be kind to your sister Margaret. She's had a sad life. I was right about Arthur Gifford. He wasn't right for her."

Another pause.

"I should like to have seen Andrew and James before I died. Of course, you will write to them. Send them, send them my love."

"Yes, of course."

James closed his eyes. He opened them again for a moment.

"Don't grieve for me," he said.

Tears came into William's eyes. His father relapsed into silence and he too sat still. Then weariness overcame him and he nearly dropped asleep.

A slight movement came from the bed. William started. He looked up at his father, in time to see a gentle smile pass over his lips. His hand fell limp. William bent forward and felt for a pulse. James was dead.

William stood for a moment looking down on the man who had been the ruling force in his life. He bent down and kissed him gently on the forehead. But it was too late. He had gone. Now William wanted only to get away from this room of death which seemed to shut him off from the rest of the world. He tiptoed to the door, as if even now a noise might wake his father, and called the servants.

Then he went downstairs and out into the garden.

(2)

All down the valley the countryside was singing of spring, the grass glistening with dew, oyster catchers piping in the distance. At that moment William was suddenly overwhelmed by the sadness of death, of his father's death, and realised that nothing would last forever, nor would he himself always be here to taste the beauty of the spring. A sense of his own mortality came upon him, and he experienced a feeling of loneliness. No other death had stirred him like this. He had just lost the person who had meant most to him in the world, and he didn't feel that his wife or children or his friends would ever quite fill that void. And in a state half waking and half in a dream, he realised that not only was he alone, but that everyone is alone in life, that there is a kind of pain in being human and feeling separate which neither friendship nor sex nor marriage can ever assuage. Love can only give the illusion of filling the gap.

"If I can die with as much courage and dignity as my father I shall be a lucky man," he told himself.

He took deep breaths of the early morning fresh air and paced up and down inconsolable. Only when one of the servants came out to persuade him to come and try to take some breakfast, did he agree to re-enter the house.

(3)

One late spring day William arrived at the company's office at Freefield accompanied by his eldest son James. Anyone seeing them together would have recognised the relationship: they shared the same line of nose, of high forehead and the way they held their heads. James had even inherited certain mannerisms of his father's in the way he spoke. The look of pride, not quite arrogance, and the confidence with which William now viewed the world, had already imprinted itself on the young man's face. Since his father's death the year before William had begun to rely heavily on his son for company during his spells home from Edinburgh, and he felt proud to have him with him. James, loved and cherished since childhood by both his parents, felt at ease in his father's company, and with William's clerk, who always treated him with respect as the owner's son.

Robert Leask was William's chief clerk down at Freefield, and William had known him for some time and felt he was a man he could trust. He often called there to see how things were going on. All the ships that berthed there came under Robert's authority, and he was also responsible for the building of boats and repairs that took place there. The head coopers, shipwrights and carpenters in charge of the bands of men who worked there, went to Robert's office when supplies arrived and he was a well-loved figure around the quays and docks.

"Good, I'm glad that's settled then," said William, referring to some matter they had discussed on which Robert needed his advice. "Send me word if you need help. We'll just go and have a look round now. Are you coming with us?"

William always enjoyed looking over Freefield. It gave him an immense satisfaction to see how well things were going, and he felt a sense of pride to know that it all belonged to him. He enjoyed meeting the men, and hearing about their work.

Robert pleaded various things he had to attend to that afternoon and so William and James left his office and made their way down to the nearest quayside, chatting as they went. The suspicion of salt in the air sharpened as they reached the water's edge, where some of the herring-boats were tied up, bobbing up and down in the water. One or two were being given a fresh coat of paint, some fishermen were on the quayside mending nets, and William lent on his cane and spoke to a group of them about the catch they had had and the prospects for the summer. He was well-known among the fishermen, who recognised Hay and Ogilvy's as a good firm to work for, and William was the sort of person who could put a name to a face and even remember details about them others would have forgotten. James acknowledged the men's deferential greeting coolly with a slight bow of the head, but seemed rather preoccupied with his own private concerns.

Turning north they skirted the edge of the dock, with more herring-boats and several tall-masted ships moored for repairs. Men were mending sails, coiling up new ropes, caulking timbers and hammering away steadily as the two men went by, eventually reaching the big sheds where fish were being cured, salted, dried, weighed and packed into barrels. William stopped to watch some of the fish being checked and pronounced himself satisfied. He saw too that there was an ample supply of barrels ready for the next week's catch, passed the time of day with the man in charge of inspecting the fish, and he and James moved on. Next came the coopers' yard. William was always fascinated to watch the coopers at work, acknowledging their skill in bending the wood in rings round the huge belly of the barrel so that they would fit. He was amazed at the number of finished barrels they turned out in one day. Here too was the yard where sawyers, carpenters and shipwrights were busy working against a noisy background of hammering, banging and sawing, of flying wood chips and sawdust and a smell of newly-seasoned timber. There was a large store of parts of skiffs brought over ready-made from Norway, and tall piles of timber to be used in shipbuilding. There were two small boats on the stocks in the process of construction, one of them almost completed, a work of satisfying craftsmanship and pleasing to the eye. Ever since he had haunted the shipyards at Aberdeen as a youth William had taken pleasure in watching boats being built, and now he had the added joy of knowing that this shipyard was his.

Further on they came to the ships' riggers and the sailmakers' shop with its odour of canvas where men were patiently stitching the heavy stiff material with large-sized needles. From there they walked on to the end of the quay that nearly closed the mouth of the dock at one end, and William declared they had seen enough.

"The herring fishing is not doing as well as I should have hoped," he said thoughtfully. "Let's hope we get a good season in June. We'll come down again next week."

"Father,' began James, as if he had kept a lot of matters pent up inside him and had to let them out. "I know how much all of this means to you. I mean, I know you want me to come home to Shetland and become part of the business. You've got it all lined up for me. I know how keen you are on the farms at Laxfirth and Veensgarth. But surely you know what life in Edinburgh is like, it's more interesting, more exciting, more rewarding than life here. I don't think I want to come up here and bury myself in the fish trade. And all the talk of whaling – it bores me."

"But I don't bury myself in the fish trade," said William, feeling hurt and angry, because it was something that did mean a great deal to him. He had dearly wanted his own son to be as closely linked in the business as he and his father had been. He was proud of his family, and especially proud of James, almost as though he was an extension of himself.

"I'm often on trips down south," he went on, "and I take an interest in a lot of other things in life. I have friends in Edinburgh and Manchester and a host of other places. They don't think I'm dull."

"Father, what I'm saying is, I want to stay in Edinburgh," said James resolutely. "At least for the time being."

He was twenty-two, with the world at his feet. William looked sharply at him, and signed inwardly. He remembered how he'd had no choice. He was made to give up university in Aberdeen and return to Lerwick to work with his father against his will. For him it had worked out, for his heart was in Shetland, and there was something that drew him back each time he went away. The warmth of close-knit relationships, the feeling of belonging in spite of the remoteness and the isolation, obviously meant more to him than it did to James. If he antagonised his son and insisted he return to Shetland against his own wishes, he might lose his friendship forever. He loved his son too dearly to take the risk.

"We'll talk about this later," he said, as they made their way back to Robert Leask's office, but he spoke with a heavy heart. For James had just shattered one of his most cherished dreams.

(4)

July 1832 was a month few Shetlanders would ever forget. It began with a cholera scare. Cholera had been raging in mainland Britain and as a precaution, all ships coming into Lerwick harbour were required to observe ten days' quarantine before their occupants were allowed to land. It had been a disappointing summer and it was a bright but blustery day when the schooner *Magnus Troil* arrived at Lerwick from Leith in the middle of the afternoon. William happened to be out on the quay at the warehouse watching goods being unloaded as the ship came into view up Bressay Sound. She was a fine sight in the sunshine with her two tall masts, surmounted by flags, her white sails billowing in the stiff breeze, and William paused to watch her as she drew near. He could see people crowding on her deck and felt sorry for them having to spend the next few days rowing round the harbour or fishing to while away the time. Later on he noted that she had dropped anchor and furled her sails and now one small boat bobbed up and down against her side, presumably that of the quarantine officer who was the only person allowed on board.

William had just passed the Tolbooth with its steeple on his way back to Hayfield when he crossed Dr Spence, one of Lerwick's surgeons, in the street.

"The *Magnus Troil* is in," called William, by way of greeting. "She'll have had a rough trip."

"I know," said Dr Spence, a large fairish man with sideboards. "The quarantine officer's just been to see me. They've got a sick man on board. The officer came to ask me to go out and see him, but I'm not going to risk it. If it's the cholera, the least contact the better."

"But if they need medical help," began William.

"I gather he's not in a desperate state," went on the doctor. "If they bring word tomorrow I'll send Dr Barclay. Don't spread the news. The people here will panic. And it hasn't yet been proved it's the cholera."

Next day Dr Barclay went on board the *Magnus Troil* with an assistant and found the man much worse. Some angry folk tried to prevent them coming ashore when they returned to the landing stage and threatened them with oaths and insults. Dr Barclay, a short little man with a paunch, sat cowering in the rowing boat, his beady eyes full of fear.

Next day the man on board the *Magnus Troil* died, the yellow flag was hauled up to the mast and the passengers and crew were condemned to ten more days' quarantine. Consternation in Lerwick ran high, because although the authorities had tried to keep the matter a secret, the news had soon leaked out.

But then an even greater danger loomed which took people's minds away from the scare of cholera. The day the man died the wind freshened and the sea was cast up into huge waves, bursting with heavy showers of spray over the little quays and up against the lodberries, the wind whistling through the shrouds of the ships in the harbour which no longer seemed to offer them any protection. As the sun disappeared the gale increased and blew with greater fury than the inhabitants, used to mighty storms, ever remembered. All night the hurricane-force wind roared across the treeless island, without ever letting-up, here and there with such force that it ripped off peat roofs and tore away slates from more substantial buildings. The relentless pounding of the surf on the shore could be heard from the inland valleys. Little boats tied up in the harbour were smashed to pieces. All thoughts were with the men out at the haaf fishing, especially those who had gone thirty to forty miles off the east coast, for with the wind from the north-west they had no chance of reaching the relative safety of a harbour. Throughout the summer night a kind of yellow glow filled the sky and the howling of the wind and sea had not abated when very early in the morning groups of anxious people, many of them women, gathered at every small landing-place. William and Charles Ogilvy were among those who fought their way against the violence of the storm, hardly able to stand upright, down to the lodberries, and talked to people trying to ascertain what was going on. Fear showed on every weary face.

"Sixty boats missing" said one, "with six men on board. Over three hundred not accounted for. It's a total disaster."

William had brought a telescope and was looking out over the harbour. "I'm amazed the *Magnus Troil* hasn't slipped her anchor," he said. He could see one or two people up on her deck. Then he focussed his sight southwards over Bressay Sound. "The revenue cutter is on its way," he said. "She'll soon be here. Maybe she has been able to pick up some survivors."

All day they lingered near the harbour for news of the fishermen. A heavy lumbering sailing ship raced into harbour, nearly colliding with the *Magnus Troil*. She had rescued six crews but had seen many other boats upside down in the water. The cutter *Swan* had also brought back two crews.

Later on a sixern appeared from the north, struggling to reach the shore. The onlookers watched the man at the helm, and three men managing the sail, raising it as each billow of surf approached and then lowering it when it had passed. Soon they could see that there were twelve men, eight lying at the bottom of the boat, worn out with exhaustion and exposure, and all of them soaked to the skin and at the limit of their endurance. As they finally reached the landing stage the tired people cheered hoarsely and rushed to help them out of the boat.

For two whole days more the wind hardly diminished. Tales of heroism and miraculous escapes began to reach the little town. Sailors from Dutch herring boats had bravely risked their lives to rescue some crews. When the final count was made, thirty-one boats had been lost, though fourteen of their crews had been picked up. One hundred and five men had lost their lives and a great number of children became orphans that day.

William shared with all Shetland the trauma of those several days. He was stunned by the human cost of what had happened, and saddened at the death of men he had known for years. But in the following days he and Charles had also to reckon up the financial cost to their firm of the hurricane. Damage at Freefield and at some of the fishing stations round the islands had been considerable, and most of the men rescued had lost their boats and their livelihood. It would put a heavy strain on Hay and Ogilvy's resources and on those of the Shetland Bank.

Such was the general heartbreak and grief that when the passengers and crew of the *Magnus Troil*, themselves very shaken by the storm, were finally allowed to land, people hardly realised that the man who had died on board had not had the cholera, and that the scare had been groundless.

(5)

William had written to both his brothers telling them of the hurricane and the loss of life and damage it had caused. In due course they both replied.

James' letter was the first to arrive from New York, where he was now established as a merchant with wife and family. His affairs seemed to be going well and he wrote of the success of his business. He gave a vivid description of the busy waterfront at New York and the fine new buildings that were going up everywhere, and he said he would find it difficult to settle back in Shetland now that he had made his life in the New World. There was obviously room for enterprise in America provided you had courage and were ready to take a risk and work hard. James had been a reserved young man and hadn't shared William's intimacy with his father. But now on the other side of the Atlantic he kept in touch by infrequent letters which depended on the availability of ships to bring them up to Edinburgh and thence to Shetland.

Andrew's letter from Singapore took far longer to reach Shetland. He now held a position of authority in the administration of the colony, had become rich and seemed satisfied with his exotic rather lonely life. He had never married, concentrated all his efforts on his career and did not seek a busy social life. Only once did he mention his housekeeper, a native woman to whom he seemed attached.

"In this hot and humid climate I sometimes think with nostalgia of our cool and windy Shetland," he wrote. "But of course I don't regret coming here. Ships call here from China, Japan, Sumatra, Java and India. There are now about a hundred Europeans and more arrive every month. Business is doing well and looks set to continue. I count myself fortunate to have watched this place grow; Chinese are now settled where at first there were mangrove swamps, the native area, which began as a fishing village, is thriving, and the town is laid out like any European settlement with fine roads and a bridge over the river. The governor insists all the natives be treated with every consideration; this has always been the policy and I myself am convinced that these good relationships have added to the success of this place."

Most news came by post. One day another letter arrived by boat from Leith with a thin black band round the envelope.

"What's this?" said William in alarm. "It's from Edinburgh." And he tore open the envelope.

The letter was brief. It came from the Edmunds, the family with whom their son James had lodged during his school years.

"Dear William," it ran,"This is to tell you the sad news that your beloved son James died yesterday of the cholera. We have made all the necessary arrangements and will be in touch with you again soon. We want to offer you our sincerest condolences and to pray that God will be with you in your sorrow."

Speechless William sat down suddenly while Margaret stood beside him, unable to digest the news. Then he raised his fists in the air and shook them in a paroxysm of rage and grief.

"No," he whispered," Not that. Not that."

And quite unable to support his wife in their joint hour of pain, he bowed his head and held his face in his hands, sinking into a melancholy from which for hours no one could rouse him.

(6)

People who knew William well said that he was never the same again after the death of his eldest son. It even seemed for a while that he lost interest in the business, and from that year onward the books of Hay and Ogilvy were not balanced. Yet he continued to invest in property, mainly financed by loans from the Bank of Scotland.

Now William had ten children; four more had been born, including Arthur James, the baby in whose care Margaret tried to bury her own grief. Two others had recently died, Arthur Gifford in infancy and five-year-old little Laurence of a wasting disease. Child mortality was common and had to be borne with stoicism. The death of a young man of twenty-four on the threshold of life with such grace and promise was far harder to come to terms with. For a while William's friends spoke of him in hushed whispers and respected his grief. He himself did his best to draw comfort from his other children; Barbara, his handsome daughter of twenty, and his sons Charles and William, both a year younger, now studying in Edinburgh. Andrew had just left school in Montrose, Anne was fifteen, John ten, George eight, Mary five and Thomas three. William loved them all, but he felt that none of them could take James' place.

Not only had shadows lengthened over William's life. The era of prosperity in Shetland was over. During the next two years there were bad harvests and the poor crofters suffered disastrously. The oats got the blight, and even the potatoes did not do well. In addition, all down the east coast of the islands the herring fishing was unproductive, fewer whalers came up to Lerwick, and the cod-fishing declined. In desperation the local people even took to stealing their neighbours' peats or fish or potatoes. The men relied on the fishing for their livelihood, and when the next winter, disease even attacked the cattle, sheep and horses, many ordinary folk were near to despair. Encouraged by the hope of a new life in America, the more enterprising began to emigrate to avoid starvation.

It was not only the very poor who were leaving Shetland. William went down one day to the harbour to say goodbye to a young cousin and his wife from Yell who had decided there was no future for them in the islands. Autumn had come early and it was a grey and chilly day with quite a swell on the water. Little groups of people arrived at the landing-stage, countrywomen in long coloured cotton dresses, with pinafores, frilled white caps on their heads and long tartan shawls round their shoulders, fishermen with long trousers and short jackets and some with their woollen caps on their heads. Surrounded by their numerous children they carried only a basket or some goods tied up in a cloth. They stood huddled together, unsmiling, clinging to their relatives and friends, waiting for the little boats to take them out to the waiting schooner anchored in the bay.

Several other families appeared, men in more formal dress and their wives in bonnets, followed by a porter with a trunk.

"I thought you'd come too late", said William with relief as a tall dark man, his pretty dark young wife and their five children joined the waiting crowds. "It's almost high tide."

"We're very tired, we've had a hellish journey," said John Smith. "I'm not looking forward to the crossing."

"They say the Atlantic can be very rough at this time of year," said his wife.

"I hope you know what you are doing," said William. "I'm sure some of these people don't. Here's a letter for my brother James in New York. He should be able to put you in touch with someone who can help you."

"I'll send a letter as soon as we arrive," promised John. "Come dear, we must go to the ship. Come children, say goodbye to Uncle William."

Words seemed totally inadequate to express their feelings when they were going to the other side of the world, not knowing what to expect or even if they would survive the journey. William and they knew full well it was unlikely they would ever see each other again.

He kissed the young wife on both cheeks and she began to weep silently. He clasped John's hand and patted him encouragingly on the shoulder.

"Good luck," he said.

They turned and got into the little boat, the last of the passengers for the emigrant ship, and William watched as they were rowed away. He stayed on the quayside as they reached the schooner and climbed up on deck, turned to wave and moved out of sight. He waited as the crew manned the yards and pulled up the anchor, and brought the ship round into the wind. The sails began to fill and then the ship began to move quickly across the bay.

William could see people on deck but they were too far away to distinguish their faces. He pulled out his white handkerchief and waved it in the air. Then, as the ship disappeared into the distance, he turned and made his way sadly back to his counting-house wondering how many more of his fellow Shetlanders would be forced to leave their native land and seek a new life overseas.

(7)

It was in 1837, when both William and Charles Ogilvy were faced with the complete collapse of the herring fishery, that Margaret, William's wife, worn out with bearing fifteen children, and emotionally drained by her son James' death, fell into a decline and died. She had not really been well for some time, but William had been so preoccupied that he had scarcely noticed that she had been growing paler, thinner and more exhausted and listless. He was not even at home when she died, having gone off to the farm at Laxfirth leaving the house in the care of the servants.

It had been too late to send a messenger and they had waited for him to return. He had thought it strange to see the servant obviously on the lookout for him as he rode up on his horse in the evening. On hearing the news he rushed into the house, leaving the man to stable his mount. It was not until he saw the tearful faces of his youngest children, and his eldest daughter came to him and threw herself into his arms weeping, that he was forced to accept the truth.

His first feelings were of guilt that Margaret had slipped away from them and he had not even been able to say goodbye. He hastened up to the bedroom where she lay still with her eyes closed.

He knelt down by the bedside, longing to ask her forgiveness. Through tears he gazed at his wife's face, calm in death, and realised how much he had loved her. Why had he been so reticent? Why had he never told her of recent years how much he cared for her? She had grown old bearing him children and being the emotional support of all the family, never resenting his close relationship with his father, nor been jealous of his special love for their son James. She had been a true companion when he needed it. Somehow he had never been grateful for all she had done. At this moment her failings faded into insignificance and he could only mourn her loss. Twenty-six years they had been married and now she was gone and he was left alone. Feelings of self-pity mingled with his grief.

He remained by the bedside for a long time until he lost track of time. Then a servant tiptoed in and whispered that they had come to lay out the body. He shook himself, rose to his feet and went downstairs to try to comfort his young family.

CHAPTER EIGHT

Omens

Not long after the death of his wife, William received a letter from Andrew in India, to say that he had decided to return to Shetland. William was surprised, as he had not expected that he would ever see either of his brothers again. The letter had taken some time to arrive and contained few details.

One day when the *Magnus Troil* had arrived from Leith, a message came that a visitor had come to see William at Hayfield. He didn't immediately attach much importance to it – perhaps it was some visiting preacher or geologist or naturalist studying the wild life of the islands who was seeking his hospitality. Then the servant showed in a tall, distinguished-looking man in a light brown jacket and breeches. Only a few moments passed before recognition dawned.

"Andrew!" he said incredulously, and they both moved forward to clasp in a tight brotherly embrace. Any childish jealousies had long since been forgotten.

William looked his brother up and down and couldn't find words to express his feelings. He called for tea and they sat down together to talk.

"What's made you come back here then?" asked William curiously. "I thought you enjoyed your life out East. It seems to have been a sudden decision."

"I suppose I wanted to see the places of my boyhood before I die," said Andrew, who seemed to have almost lost his Shetland accent. "However far you go you don't realise how much those early years impress on you. I've been cut off from all the people I knew, the places I loved. Somehow as you get older, they seem to matter more."

But although his curly hair was greying, he looked surprisingly young for his age.

"Things change here too," said William gently. "Don't expect to find everything as when you went away. People have died and things are different. I've been here all the time, and I've seen many changes."

"That's not what I'm afraid of," said Andrew as he drank his tea. "I need to rediscover the world of my boyhood, as it was then. To recognise all the things that made me the person I am. Call it a crisis of identity if you like."

"You never married," remarked William.

"It was a man's world in Singapore," said Andrew. "There were four times as many European men as women, and most of the women were married when they came out there. I suppose the nearest I got to marriage was to marrying my housekeeper, but it's just not done. She was a native woman and I was very attached to her. I've left her well provided for. She could never have come back with me to Shetland."

"It's different for me," said William. "I've had a wife and a large family. But when your partner dies you're left very much on your own. I've got the responsibility of nine children. It's different for you as a bachelor. Perhaps you will say I've had the better part."

"Who knows?" said Andrew. "We're each given a portion not the whole of life. And it's never the same as the next person's."

"Come and see the children," said William, getting up. "If you're staying long we shall hope to see a lot of you."

"I am thinking of taking a house in Lerwick and staying for the next few months," said Andrew.

"You can stay here as long as you like till you get settled," said William.

(2)

Andrew took a house in Lerwick, and to William's surprise, seemed satisfied for a while to live with a servant, getting to know local society. He had amassed a fortune, and had brought back from the East all kinds of treasures and souvenirs that fascinated local visitors.

One of the first people he got to know was Dr Edmonston, an amiable bachelor of about his own age, who had lodgings in one of the apartments in Fort Charlotte, now vacated by the garrison and let to local residents. Dr Edmonston came from the island of Unst, and had a wealth of knowledge about Shetland, having written a book about it. He was not only a competent doctor, but also a pleasant and intelligent man, who had travelled to Paris and Rome. He could exchange stories with Andrew and enjoy his descriptions of life in Singapore, and the people he had met, including the founder, Sir Stamford Raffles, during Raffles' short stay not long after he had arrived there. Raffles' ideas of a free-trading city, strategically placed on the way to China, and run on human and enlightened principles, had inspired Andrew. His departure had coincided with the appointment of a new governor in 1837, whose outlook he did not share.

Another acquaintance was James Duncan, a merchant who lived outside Lerwick not far from Hayfield, where he had even managed to cultivate a small plantation of trees. He had an incisive mind and a great wit and was very good company.

94

During the winter the two surgeons, Dr Spence and Dr Barclay, were often of the party. Dr Spence was a hearty, easy-going fellow who laughed at his own jokes. Dr Barclay was a much more timid gentleman who was brother to the local minister and knew a lot of people. Sometimes William and Charles Ogilvy joined them. Many times they spent drinking, smoking, and exchanging tales to while away the long dark winter evenings.

The only person who did not seem to take to Andrew was Charles Ogilvy. Charles had been a child when Andrew left Shetland for good and hardly remembered him. Although Charles had never had quite the same intimacy with William as his father had done, he seemed to resent Andrew's appearance on the scene, taking up a lot of William's time. It made William sad, and he was annoyed when Charles referred to Andrew as "your nabob brother." It was the first of a number of differences that were eventually to drive a wedge between them.

Andrew enjoyed going up to Laxfirth to spend time angling and seemed to like his own company. He took a long boat trip up to West Sandwick in Yell, where John Ogilvy, Charles' brother, lived. He had sold up his share in the business some time ago, and now lived the life of a country gentleman, with a large mansion, excellent stables and a farm where he practised improvements with fine cattle and mixed-breed sheep. Andrew also went down to see the deepwater quays Hay and Ogilvy's had had built at Scalloway, and down the coast to see John Bruce, the laird at Sandlodge he remembered as a boy.

It seemed to William that his brother was looking for something, something he had apparently lost out East and thought he could find here in Shetland. Although he talked of going down to Edinburgh, he constantly postponed his journey. It was almost as if having spent all his life living to the full and never pausing to reflect, he now needed extra space to put things into perspective. While the fact of their being blood relations and having been brought up together counted for a great deal, so that they knew each others' reactions better than that of a casual friend, yet William had to admit to himself that in many areas of life his brother was almost a total stranger to him.

But there was always the hope of their new relationship blossoming into friendship, and becoming a new intimacy, and William welcomed his brother's arrival and company so soon after the death of his wife.

(3)

Two years after Andrew's return from the Far East, Charles Ogilvy, who was now not only chief magistrate for Lerwick, but vice-consul for Denmark, received a letter from the governor of the island of Faroe to the west of Shetland, which belonged to Denmark. Christian Ployen proposed to come to

Shetland to study the island's economy, the fishing and the agriculture, with a view to improving conditions on Faroe.

At the beginning of June William stood with Charles Ogilvy at the top of the hewn stone steps that led down to the water from the quayside in Lerwick, to greet him as he came ashore from his ship in a rowing boat. Mr Ployen was tall, fair and blue-eyed, very dignified and spoke excellent English. Three other men accompanied him. After they had shaken hands and said a few words, Charles took them out of town to Seafield to meet his family, before leaving them at Lerwick's only hotel where they were to stay.

That evening Mr Ployen dined with William and other guests, and after the meal when the decanters were passed round, and the men were left to talk together, they made plans to give him a comprehensive tour of Shetland. William was impressed with Mr Ployen's knowledge, good humour and his eagerness to learn all he could during his stay. For his part William was determined to get on good terms with him, because business with Faroe could grow out of such a relationship.

During his stay, William, Mr Ployen and his three companions set off one early fine morning to visit the fishing stations at Scalloway and on the island of Burra. The hills above Lerwick were purple with heather as they rode off on their ponies. Three Lerwick porters went with them to carry their luggage.

Outside Lerwick they met calvacades of ponies carrying men, women and children going out to cut their peats. Where the peats were being dug the moors were full of dark scars or the piles of thick sods that had been removed to reach the fuel underneath.

They went up the track up part of the Tingwall valley, where gulls and sheep were the only life to be seen, and eventually came out on the hillside above Scalloway, with a wide view of the sea and the many islands out to the west. A lot was going on in the harbour with fishing sloops and larger vessels loading unloading and preparing to leave. William took his visitors to see the small store which Hay and Ogilvy's had established there, which sold many of the goods they imported. Without realising it, William talked with real enthusiasm of the many concerns which absorbed his daily life and passed on this enthusiasm to his listeners. Here, he pointed out, there was everything from scythes to spades, cooking equipment, fishing gear and all kinds of clothing; casks of gin and whisky, great sacks of oatmeal, coffee, tea, sugar, sailors' knives, candles and soap, stacked altogether in delightful disarray. The shopkeeper leaned out over the counter in front of his goods and smiled respectfully as a large sleek black cat strolled in from the inner room. With the quayside nearby and fish cellars next door, rats and mice were an everyday pest and the cat was kept busy.

Then they went to inspect the large stone quay with its warehouses where larger boats could unload and load, the fish stores and the coopers' yard.

"We'll push on to Burra while the weather's good," said William as they took their leave.

The tawny hump-backed islands of Burra stretched out in the sunlight beyond the harbour of Scalloway, and there were several wide stretches of water to be rowed across before they could reach the fishing station that William had brought his visitors to see. Six sturdy oarsmen rowed them over the sea, keeping up a steady pace and scarcely pausing to rest.

Even before they reached the beach on Burra a strong smell of fish pervaded the air. A scene of unusual activity greeted them.

It was a wide sloping beach composed of large flat stones, and along the top were rows of stone huts, roofed with straw thatch, where the fishermen lived for the season while they were ashore. Beyond were the fish curers' huts and a store run by Hay and Ogilvy's to supply the men with all they needed. Piles of fish rose from the beach, and much of the fish was laid out flat on the stones to dry. Women and old men were making more piles or turning the fish in the sun.

Salting vats, washing troughs, triangles and beams where the fish was weighed were scattered over the shore, and the fish curer walked about keeping an eye on the work. Down nearer the water's edge sixerns and smaller boats were hauled up on the shingle, some just arriving with fish, others preparing to go to sea. Men were drying their lines or just standing about with folded arms talking in huddles. Others were busy cooking over a fire.

William explained the busy scene to Mr Ployen and his companions. The three men were to receive training in fish curing during their stay.

"The fishermen come here from May till August," he began. "Each day when the fish is landed it has first to be cleaned, the head removed, the liver removed and saved for oil, and the backbone split so that the cod will lie flat. Next they stack the fish and cover each layer with salt. Only the fish split on the same day can be salted together so that it is known how long it has been 'in salt.' If too much salt is added then the fish becomes 'burnt' and if not enough, then it might rot. It's a skillful job to determine just how much salt will be required to preserve it."

"After a day or two the salt works its way into the fish, and then the excess is washed off and the cod placed in large piles to drain for two or three days. Then it is dried in the sun on the beach. They turn the fish over regularly to make sure the excess moisture dries off. When the weather's bad it's all covered with tarpaulins."

"The final stage is grading for size and quality. The grading is very important because the quality determines the price of the fish, and the fishermen are paid a percentage of the money received from the catch. You also need to know the requirements of the market, some parts of Europe favour a particular quality or style of cure."

"Shall we go and have a word with the fish curer?" proposed William. He told Mr Ployen that during the summer when the men were engaged in fishing and fish curing, the women were left to care for the crofts, tend the crops and look after the animals.

"After August the beach will be wholly deserted till next spring," he said.

The Danish governor was immensely interested in all that he saw, for he grasped that much of what was being done here could be carried out in his own island.

Later William took him to Freefield and showed him some of the fleet of a hundred or so half-decked boats that Hay and Ogilvy's owned or managed. In the cooperage department Mr Ployen was somewhat alarmed at the huge number of barrels in store, in case the fishing should decline and the firm be left with a surplus on their hands. Mr Ployen also made another remark that William would later remember. William invited him to Laxfirth and showed him all the innovations he had introduced on his farm. Mr Ployen said openly he could not see William getting any return for his expenses for many years to come. But his remarks fell on deaf ears.

William explained how he had been encouraging his tenants to use a fixed rotation of crops, but some of them were not being co-operative.

"It's not just the money," he said. "It's the difficulties with the tenants. If they don't comply I shall turn them out."

Before Mr Ployen set out for a visit to mainland Scotland William invited him to come back to Laxfirth for some angling. In addition, he discussed with him the possibility of sending cod sloops to Faroe to explore the opportunities for fishing.

Altogether William found the governor a very entertaining companion.

(4)

The following summer William married off his two daughters: Barbara, the elder, to the son of Henry Cheyne of Tangwick, an up and coming young lawyer in Edinburgh, and Anne, the younger one, to Andrew Humphrey of Reawick, son of a landowner who was another progressive farmer. He was related to William's father. It was a happy time, when the cares of business could be forgotten, and family and friends could join together in celebration. Now, with Charles and William living in Edinburgh, Andrew and John having begun careers with a merchant firm in Calcutta, six of his children had now left home.

William was now fifty-three and it was three years since his wife had died. His thick curly hair was grey, but he enjoyed good health. After the weddings were over, he spent some time down in Edinburgh, enjoying social occasions and meeting old friends.

He had come with a definite idea in mind. Seeing his daughters' happiness, and thinking too that it would be good for his younger children to have a new mother, longing too for another companion with whom to share his life, he had resolved to marry again. He made up his mind to visit some old friends of his father's in Glasgow, including Margaret Scott, a pretty widow of thirty-four whom he had often admired. They had both lost a partner; both had had to cope with bereavement, both had to find a new life. Would she still be free to marry, and would she consent to marry him? Would she have the courage to leave the mainland and take on his own youngsters?

He travelled by express barge from Edinburgh to Glasgow, catching glimpses of the new railway line under construction on the way. He pondered as the barge made its leisurely way through the countryside from one lock to the next at the pace of the patient horses. It made little sound as it slid through the water and William preferred to watch the landscape placidly pass by rather than talk to his boisterous companions.

The journey took over ten hours and he had plenty of time to reflect. He realised that he felt as reticent as a youngster courting for the first time did. Would he frighten her off if he proposed to her during his short visit? But there wasn't any time to waste. He decided to sound out a mutual acquaintance, who thoroughly applauded his plan, and encouraged him to approach her directly.

Margaret seemed conscious that he had taken extra pains with his appearance, in his immaculate dark coat with tails and a wide white silk tie. She herself had chosen a dove-coloured dress that showed her dark hair and complexion off to its best advantage.

"We've always been good friends," he began, as her brother tactfully left them together. "Now that we're both alone, I was wondering." He paused, uncertain how to go on as he saw a flush of colour come to her cheek. "I was wondering whether you had enough fondness for me to consider becoming my wife. I know it will mean a complete change for you to come up to Shetland and maybe you are not willing to give up your comfortable existence here and risk a life in the far north with me. But we are not totally cut off, and I come down south quite often. Will you consider it?"

"William, I hadn't imagined for one moment that this was why you had come to see me," said Margaret, both flattered and delighted, for she had always considered William attractive. "Believe me, I have always had a very high regard for you. Perhaps I should say affection," she said, blushing again.

"Does this mean you say yes?" asked William, his heart filling with sudden joy. "That you accept me?"

Margaret was almost inclined to smile at the earnestness of his expression.

"We never know where life is going to lead us," she said courageously. "But I think I can truthfully say that if you ask me to become Mrs Hay, then I shall wholeheartedly accept."

William beamed; then, leaning forward he put his arms round her and kissed her gently.

The wedding was arranged in Glasgow at the earliest possible moment. William wrote to his children in high spirits telling them of his marriage and how Margaret had agreed to come up to Shetland and live with them.

Hopefully a new era in his personal life was about to begin.

(5)

Several important matters awaited William on his return.

His frustration with his tenants at Laxfirth had reached such a pitch that he decided the only solution was to clear the arable land of dwellings and force the crofters to move onto new crofts on another part of the estate a mile or two away. He was not heartless enough to turn them off with nowhere to go, and indeed had actually been sufficiently considerate to have a local school built and provided a schoolmaster. He also chose the summer time to carry out his plans, mainly because it suited him to have the ground cleared in readiness for the next season, but it did mean that the crofters would not be moving out in the most cold and inclement weather.

One day he and John Swanson, his foreman, rode out on horseback down to see that the evictions had indeed taken place. The huddle of crofts stood together in the valley, miserable dwellings made of stone walls put together without mortar, filled with clay or mud, and roofed with layers of sods which gave them an uneven, unkempt appearance. On one side of the low entrance that led to the living room, were the byre for the animals and a barn where work could be done indoors in winter.

As they drew near William was incensed to see that a funnel of smoke was still escaping from one of the roofs.

"I gave orders that everyone should leave," he said angrily. "Who is still left behind? Go and see."

John Swanson dismounted from his horse and pushed his way into the croft. When he came out a few minutes later he came over to William and said, "It's an old woman. She refuses to go. What shall I do?"

Pursing his lips, William got down from his horse, flung his reins over its neck and strode into the dwelling, John Swanson close behind him. William almost shuddered at the squalor of the interior, blackened by soot, with very little inside except an old woman lying on a pallet on the earthen floor, and a dark, wild-eyed young man kneeling beside her.

"Come mother, you can't stay here," he pleaded urgently, as William entered without ceremony.

"I expressly asked that anyone unable to walk should be given every assistance," he said. "Why is this woman still here?"

"She just won't go," said the young man rather desperately. "I can't move her. She says it's her home and she's not going. The rest of the family has gone."

The woman turned her face to the wall and seemed to be ignoring what was being said.

William's temper snapped. "Set fire to the roof," he said curtly. "Then she'll have to go. Make her see that it's a far better place she's going to."

He turned on his heel and walked out. John Swanson's face was stern as he addressed the pair.

"Come woman," he said, seizing her by the arm but speaking not unkindly. "You heard what Mr Hay said. You'll burn to death if you stay here."

Tears streaming down her face, the old woman rose with difficulty to her feet and, leaning on her son's arm, hobbled to the entrance. They had scarcely emerged when John Swanson took a torch from the peat fire and set fire to the roof. Within minutes it was burning merrily as the evicted pair moved slowly away.

William, standing by his horse, watched them go.

"I don't understand," he said to John as he joined him. "Why on earth should she want to stay in that terrible old hovel?"

John, used to dealing with the crofters and having more insight into their poverty-stricken lives, replied simply, "She's always lived here. It was her home."

(6)

But for William catastrophe was looming ahead. If Mr Ployen, an intelligent outside observer bent on studying Shetland's economy, had expressed concern over the state of Hay and Ogilvy's business and seen bad omens for the future, William himself was reluctant to face the facts. Several years of bad harvests, poor fishing and overspending had led him and Charles to grant themselves extensive loans from the Shetland Bank, and quite recently to seek more advances from the Royal Bank of Scotland. While William was down south celebrating his marriage, the early fishing had failed, and in September there was another severe gale that caused great damage and wrecked some of the herring boats.

For two years they struggled on, but it became increasingly clear that disaster was in sight. William, like his father, was always prepared to take a risk and he had been recklessly extravagant, trusting that the firm would pull through.

But one morning in June 1842, William sat in his study at Hayfield; a quiet sanctuary lined with dark bookshelves. It overlooked the garden, and the scent of honeysuckle wafted in through the open window and birds sang outside. William could hear young Meg's childish cries of delight as she played with her nurse somewhere in the distance. Such a glorious day would have aroused hope and optimism in most people. But William's mood was far from happy. News had just arrived that the Royal Bank had refused the loan they had asked for. Finances were in such a state that this was a severe blow. And a letter from his son Charles in Edinburgh expressed his fears not only for the firm of Hay and Ogilvy's, but also for all the people who relied on them for their livelihood. It was worded so strongly that William could not fail to see the implications. He groaned and held his head in his hands, as if he had just seen clearly for the first time the impossible position he was in. All those unbalanced books, all that careless living, had led to this.

His father had once accused him of being too ambitious. He had always had positive plans for himself in life that sounded feasible to his mind. He had let nothing stand in his way, other people's demands or feelings, and only success had mattered to him. He had to admit that success had been sweet. But now the day of reckoning had come.

What options were left? In a last desperate attempt to save the situation William made up his mind to go personally to Edinburgh, offer the remainder of his personal property to the Royal Bank as security, and beg them to grant him one more loan. But he knew that it was too late.

When he did go to Edinburgh, he carried with him a letter from himself and Charles Ogilvy, authorising his son-in-law Henry Cheyne to apply for the sequestration of their personal estates. The firm of Hay and Ogilvy was to be taken over by trustees. It was the worst possible humiliation for a merchant. William was effectively bankrupt.

CHAPTER NINE

Failure

There was a calm sea with only a light breeze as William journeyed back from Aberdeen to Lerwick. He had travelled from Edinburgh up to Aberdeen by coach in order to save a few precious hours, his mind not on the constant jolting of the vehicle, the frequent stops to change horses, the pleasantries of his fellow travellers, but on the predicament he was now in. It was always in his thoughts as the ship made its way up the north coast of Scotland, and instead of seeking out other passengers, as he usually did, in the hopes perhaps of one day doing business with them, he now shunned their company. After a light meal of ship's biscuit and a little spirits, he stayed up on deck, watching the thin blue rib of land that was Sunderland drop away in the distance to the west. It was evening and the sun shone on the silver sea, catching the tumble of foam as each wave broke in long lines over the tranquil water.

He now recognised the warnings a number of people had tried to give him about overstretching Hay and Ogilvy's resources. But he had been too arrogant. Most of the expansion that had taken place at Freefield and at Scalloway had provided badly needed employment, but had been done with borrowed money. Most of his newly acquired land had been bought with loans he could no longer hope to repay. If matters had been handled differently, he felt the situation they now found themselves in could have been avoided. For this William blamed Charles Ogilvy and it made him feel bitter towards him. He was almost glad that his wife Margaret had been spared the rift that was bound to grow up between them.

It was true they had not been prudent in borrowing so much capital from the Shetland Bank. Some of all this could have been averted. The failure of the bank would not just affect Hay and Ogilvy's – all of their employees, most of the coopers, shipwrights and carpenters who worked at Freefield, even people like Robert Leask, would lose their jobs. All those fishermen who relied on the firm at Scalloway and elsewhere to sell their fish, and whose modest savings had been deposited with the bank would lose all they had. Captains of the boats that plied for the firm up and down the coast with salted fish and other cargoes would have to find new employment. Hay and Ogilvy's had been the most successful and the most important trading firm in the islands. There was already poverty in Shetland; now many people would be desperate. Some of them would no doubt blame him and his partner for their misfortune. A sense of guilt was a heavy burden to bear on top of his own problems.

He was only gradually beginning to realise just what bankruptcy would mean to him. He would lose all his property, as both partners were liable for the firm's debts. Laxfirth, Veensgarth, Dale, Hayfield, his house and warehouse in Lerwick, the shop, he would have to sell them all. He had lost all the property that his father James had passed on to him, all that his father had striven for throughout his life. And what of his family? Where were they to live? He still had a wife and five dependent children, to care for; including little Meg, the daughter Margaret Scott had given him the previous year. He had neglected his responsibilities, and left them all vulnerable, and for this he hated himself. He brooded up on deck through the light summer night, only retiring down below when thoroughly exhausted.

It was a bright but chilly early morning as the ship made its way up Bressay Sound and into Lerwick Harbour. When William reached the quayside Charles Ogilvy was there to greet him. He looked grim.

William, unsmiling, looked pale and weary. "There was nothing I could do. We've been declared bankrupt for sixty thousand pounds. But Charles, if you had listened to me, none of this might ever have happened."

"That's not altogether fair," began Charles, but William turned on his heel and moved away, cutting short their conversation. Recriminations wouldn't help matters. It was too late.

(2)

William's face told the whole story when he reached Hayfield.

"There's nothing more to be hoped for. I'm bankrupt," he said dully.

"Then we are destitute?" asked Margaret in alarm.

"I tried to keep it from you. I went on expecting something to happen: the Bank of Scotland to issue another loan; a better year's fishing, anything. But now it's official. I know it's a terrible shock for you. But we shan't be absolutely destitute. My brother will help for a start. We'll be able to keep one of the smaller houses in Lerwick."

"But we have to leave Hayfield?" said Margaret weakly.

"I'm afraid so," said William, brusquely. "I've lost almost everything. We shall have to change our way of living. Get used to doing without things we took for granted."

"I've had an inkling for some time that there was something badly wrong," said Margaret. "You've been acting rather strangely lately."

Margaret herself was pregnant for the second time and not feeling at all well.

"I expect we shall manage," she said wanly. And then courageously," We shall bear it together."

Her spirit revived him and after he had eaten he began to plan the next step forward. Servants at Laxfirth, Hayfield and other properties in Yell and Whalsay, and many other employees, would have to lose their jobs. There would be endless letters to write. And the most pressing task was to go down to see Robert Leask, call a meeting and confront the men.

(3)

It was not something he was looking forward to. He had taken his duties as a landowner and employer seriously and enjoyed contact with the fishermen and workers; their deference and respect flattered him. He could not foresee what their reaction would be when he told them their labour was no longer needed.

Next afternoon, a restless crowd of men, some of them still with their tools in their hands, with aprons splodged with tar or chips of sawdust in their hair, others in sailors' jackets and woollen caps on their heads, had assembled on the quayside at Freefield. Disquieting rumours were already passing from mouth to mouth, that William Hay had come back from Scotland looking very worried, that men were about to be laid off, that new working practices were about to be introduced, that wages were going to be cut. But as William and Robert walked uneasily down the quay and stood up above them on a makeshift soapbox, none of them had quite imagined the seriousness of the news they were about to hear.

The chattering died away and the men turned to face William, grouped in little huddles. There was a moment or two's pause as he stood there summoning up all his courage and perhaps seeking some way of softening the blow.

"I'm afraid I have some very bad news," he began. "Bad news for us all. Hay and Ogilvy's have been declared bankrupt. The Shetland Bank has collapsed. Everything is lost. I know that many of you had savings with the bank. There's nothing anyone can do."

There was a stunned silence. You could hear the lapping of the waves against the quayside, and the flapping of the shrouds in boats moored nearby. Then, "And what about our jobs?" came a voice. "What is to happen to us?" said another.

Immediately there was uproar. An explosion of oaths, of raised fists, men with tears in their eyes. William had seldom seen tough Shetland men weep.

Robert Leask raised his hand and begged them to listen.

Expectantly, as if there was still some hope left, they quietened down.

105

William began again.

"This is a disaster for us all," he said, picking his words carefully. "I shall have to sell all my property and leave Hayfield. The shops and the business will be sold. Hay and Ogilvy's have gone into trusteeship. I can't guarantee any of you your jobs. Mr Leask will settle up with you as far as is possible. I'm very sorry," he ended lamely.

He stepped down and walked back up to the office, head bowed, shoulders hunched, shorn of all his pride, and feeling utterly wretched, leaving the men besieging Robert with questions he didn't know how to answer.

(4)

Next day William rode up through the little hamlet of Sound to visit Charles Ogilvy at Seafield. He was still feeling very bitter towards Charles, angry, humiliated and resentful. The only way to satisfy himself was to have it out with him and tell him what he thought.

The solid, well-built house at Seafield was considerably more imposing than Hayfield and Charles as chief magistrate of the district lived in comfort. But William had no time this morning for social niceties. He dismounted abruptly and marched up the staircase where the servant who knew him well, looked frightened at his burning eyes and air of determination.

"I've come to see Mr Ogilvy," he said curtly. "Tell him it's urgent."

"Yes sir."

She let him into the wide hall and went off to find her master.

After a moment or two Charles came down the stairs, pale and noticeably shaken by all that had happened.

"William," he said warmly, holding out his hand. "I'm glad..."

But William didn't let him finish.

"We've a lot to discuss," he said almost rudely, cutting him short. "Is there somewhere we can talk undisturbed?"

Charles looked taken aback. William's attitude took him by surprise and alarmed him.

"Yes, of course. Come into my study," he said, leading the way.

"Let me get you a drink," he said as they went into a room lined with leather-bound books. But William remained standing by the full-length window. It looked out onto the garden where clumps of honeysuckle trailed over the brick walls, but William's mind was on other things. He turned and faced Charles.

"How could you let this happen?" he asked accusingly.

"I?" said Charles. "Surely we are in this together?"

"All I know is that my land and property are forfeit, my business ruined and my prospects nil," said William bitterly. "And it's all your fault."

Charles looked puzzled at this sudden attack.

"William, I assure you I did all I could," he said in a conciliatory tone. "We've just been unlucky since the hurricane, bad harvests, poor fishing, and a run of misfortune. You can't blame me for all that. And please sit down and let's discuss matters civilly."

"How can I discuss matters civilly after what has happened?" blustered William, remaining where he was. "When I went into partnership with your father I didn't think it would end like this."

"Just what are you accusing me of?" asked Charles weakly, sitting down with his hand to his head.

"My estate could have paid every creditor, every creditor," roared William, "only you insisted on the company being wound up by itself. I told you at the time but you wouldn't listen."

"William, I thought it was for the best," said Charles imploringly. "Now we have to decide what we can salvage for the future."

"And you have nothing else to say?" said William seething, refusing to calm down. "I came here expecting at least an apology."

"Why should I apologise?" said Charles, standing up again, his own temper beginning to rise. "What gives you the right to come here and vent your spleen on me? We're partners; we're in this mess together. We've both borrowed too much money from the Shetland Bank and we took more than it could support. We're both responsible for what has happened."

"We may have been partners," said William, as coldly as he could. "And I married your sister. But we're not partners any more. I'm glad she didn't live to see this day. From now on we go our separate ways."

And not waiting for Charles to answer, William strode out of the room.

He felt even worse as he rode back than when he had come. His anger started to turn in on himself. He began to relive the interview between him and Charles in his own mind, and suddenly realised his partner was just as shattered as he was; though he expressed it differently. William had vented all his own bitterness on Charles, and it wasn't entirely his fault. His mind went back to the day he had taken the Danish governor round the premises at Freefield. "Aren't you overstretching yourselves?" he had seemed to say. But William had taken absolutely no notice; he had carried on business as usual, continued to borrow heavily, refused to see the warning signs. He was just as responsible as Charles was. Perhaps more so, for he was the senior partner.

He had never had a row with Charles before. Charles was easy-going like his father. Now William had said some unforgivable things, lost control of himself and created a gulf between them that would take a long time to heal. His conscience began to stir uneasily and he began to wonder what, if anything, he could do to mend the situation.

(5)

Of all the property he had now to renounce, it seemed hardest to leave Hayfield. That was where he had spent happy summer days with his eldest son, his first wife and his elder children now grown up and moved away. Those left at home, George, thirteen, Mary, ten, Thomas, nine, and Arthur, six, together with baby Meg, had known no other home. It was a bewildering time for everyone, with William often short-tempered or absent-minded. Three of the servants they had known nearly all their lives had been given notice, and preparations were made to move into a much smaller house in Lerwick not far from the new church on the outskirts of the town. There was a great deal of heart-searching as to what they could and couldn't take with them, and William looked forward to the move with foreboding.

There was almost a sense of doom hanging over the family when the day came to leave. William watched Margaret and the children drive off from Hayfield for the last time in a gig drawn by Shetland ponies. Then he went slowly up the staircase to his front door to confer with the one remaining servant about the removal of their goods, which were to follow them, and the disposal of the rest.

He paced from room to room, reliving past memories of happy prosperous times when he had arrogantly believed that life could never go wrong for him. How he had taken everything for granted, never given thanks, never stopped to think of other people's misfortunes! What a closed, selfish, personal world he had lived in! He suddenly thought of all the men who had lost their jobs, many of them honest working men, probably at this moment facing a fate far worse than his. Because he was a prosperous merchant and they were labouring men or fishermen, he had never really classed himself in the same category as them. Suddenly he saw that life was much the same for everyone, high or low. He had mistakenly allowed himself to think that he deserved his prosperity, that it was his right in life. At that moment the memory of the old woman at Laxfirth who had refused to leave the hovel where she had spent all her life came into his mind. He had genuinely thought she would be better off in a new croft several miles away. Now at last he realised the anguish he had caused her. She must have felt the very same pain that he was experiencing on leaving Hayfield, the

108

home that had marked the height of his success. Only for him it was not just leaving his home, it was turning his back on all it represented for him – money, position and prestige.

He went outside and wandered aimlessly round the garden in a state of heightened emotion and awareness. He felt as if his head would burst. Then taking a grip on himself, he went indoors again, said goodbye to the servant, and prepared to go into town.

(6)

It was never clear whether it was the upheaval and emotions of the disaster, the exhaustion of the move or simply some physical disability that caused Mrs Hay to have a miscarriage. Unable to summon any more grief at the loss of yet another child, William did sympathise with his wife's distress and felt sad when she seemed unable to recover and became a semi-invalid. It was just one more blow to add to the rest.

One morning in early autumn he escaped from the house and made his way down to the harbour. He passed the customs house and a little knot of people outside the circulating library, who stopped talking and looked the other way as he passed. Women with yokes and pails were waiting and chatting at the pump in the middle of the main street, which served the whole town and provided supplies of water for visiting shipping. Further along he saw Mr Ross the collector of taxes come out of one of the stores and was going across the street to greet him. Very pointedly the man crossed over ahead of him in order to avoid him and went on his way. William suddenly realised with pain that in some circles at least he was now despised for being a bankrupt, and was being shunned by local society.

Further on he came upon a couple of the street women who fawned on the sailors when they were in port, and a group of men reeling with drink and making lewd and loud remarks. On the corner of one of the steep alleyways that rose from the main street, stood a young girl and boy in rags and with bare feet, who begged him for money. William sighed and gave them each a small coin, for which they seemed inordinately grateful. Down by the harbour the town crier was announcing the departure of the next ship for Leith, and fishermen from small boats, porters and unemployed men hoping for a mornings' work, lounged about the little quaysides.

Although William seemed to feel an increased awareness of the struggles of other people's lives, he felt strangely cut off. He could no longer compete in the way he was used to; society no longer had a part for him to play. He was forbidden to trade or carry on any sort of business. It was as if he didn't exist.

He wanted to cry out for sympathy, but his wife was ailing and their one servant was finding it difficult to cope. The children, used to more space and more entertainment than he could offer them at the moment, were becoming very demanding, and that morning he had received a bleary note from his brother-in-law in Busta to say that his sister Margaret was so concerned about William's bankruptcy that she seemed to have lost her wits. At that moment he felt very lonely, thinking back to those serene days down south only two years ago, when he had courted his second wife, and the hopes he had brought back for the future. Why had everything suddenly turned against him? Would he ever be able to win through?

News had reached him only last week of one of his most trusted carpenters at Freefield who in desperation at being unable to feed his family had made their plight even worse by taking his own life. There was always the temptation to opt out, give way to despair, and end one's existence. That was not William's way, he was a fighter, and his family responsibilities only spurred him on. But at age fifty-four, when he should have been beginning to take things easily, to be faced with the prospect of starting business all over again, was a very bitter blow.

(7)

William was so wrapped up in his own sombre thoughts, that he didn't see David Nicolson, a friend and fellow merchant approaching. David had suffered like everyone else from the crisis in Shetland's economy caused by the failure of Hay and Ogilvy's, but he was a genuine friend and his greeting showed no embarrassment.

"I heard you had to move," he said. "I am terribly sorry."

William told him his new address and invited him to accompany him home.

"I'm afraid things are a bit different." he apologised. "I've only got a tiny room as a study and it's never very quiet. It's full of correspondence, ledgers and the like from the counting-house, as well as my books. We have to be grateful we're not out on the street."

They walked back together.

"This is a difficult matter," began David, ensconced in a cane-backed chair by the fireplace opposite William seated at the table. "I don't really know how to begin. Your brother Andrew wants to marry my eldest daughter.

William gasped with astonishment. "But how old is she? Barely eighteen? And he's fifty-two!"

"Yes," said David. "From my point of view I can see it's a good match. But Andrew is old enough to be her father. She's so young and she's quite besotted with him."

"Andrew's an attractive fellow," said William thoughtfully. "He's rich and he's got the added attraction of having been out East. I'm surprised in a way that something like this hasn't happened before."

"What am I to do?" asked David desperately. "If I tell her she can't marry him, she's crazy enough to run off and live with him. And if I go and see him and prevent the marriage, she'll never forgive me. I lose in any case."

"Leave it with me," said William, almost glad to have someone else's problem to deal with to take his mind off his own. "I'll go and see my brother and find out what his intentions are. He never spoke to me of settling down. I was under the impression he came back to see Shetland before he dies."

At the earliest opportunity William confronted his brother at his home, sitting on a couch with a dangerous-looking Javanese sword hanging from the wall above them.

"Andrew, is this true?" he began warily, not wanting to intrude on his brother's feelings. "That you intend to marry Mary Nicolson?"

Andrew paused as if he didn't know what to say. He stared out of the window into the sunshine, at the placid harbour in the distance, with the masts of several sailing ships and the lodberries extending out into the water.

"Yes," he replied finally. "I'm in love with her. Madly in love," he added sheepishly.

"Are you sure you know what you are doing" asked William earnestly. "Are you sure you want to get married at your age? After being a bachelor all these years?"

Andrew smiled wryly. "All the more reason," he said. "I never thought I should meet anyone more likely to make me happy. And let's face it, William, you were fifty-two when you married again."

"My wife was thirty-four, and a widow," said William. "She knew her own mind. Mary Nicolson, she's almost a child."

"She's not a child at eighteen, she's a very beautiful young woman," said Andrew. "In addition she's a lovely personality. And she loves me."

"And what will she do when you are an old man?" asked William with exasperation, feeling he was losing the battle. "Or if you die?"

"Then I hope as a beautiful young widow she will have a second chance," said Andrew firmly. "William, it's no use. You won't change my mind. I'm determined to make her a devoted husband."

He began to talk of other things.

In due course Andrew and Mary were married and settled in Lerwick, though Andrew's income allowed them to travel south often and move in the best society.

William felt that with his own affairs in such chaos, Andrew could perhaps have chosen a better moment. But when he saw the two of them together and how engrossed they were in each other, he could only wish them every happiness.

CHAPTER TEN

New Beginnings

"**D**ear Father", ran the letter from William's son Charles in Edinburgh, not long after the disaster which hit Hay and Ogilvy's and left the economy of Shetland in ruins. "Your news was a shock but not unexpected. William and I had often wondered how much longer the firm could run on borrowed capital. I understand your disappointment and frustration at no longer being able to trade. We both want to do all we can to help in this emergency. I shall come up to Lerwick at the earliest opportunity to see what we can do. William plans to do the same and will be writing soon." The letter ended with family greetings.

Both Charles and William were now twenty-seven and had some experience of business in Edinburgh. Their father was extremely fortunate that they were not only free to come north but were willing to do all they could to help him. Both young men were tall and fair, unlike their father, and they did not share his good looks. But their loyalty to William was strong. They came up together in the *Magnus Troil*, Charles with his wife Jessica and their three young children. They had a stormy passage in late autumn, and William met them on the quayside as they came ashore. Charles and William were struck by William's obvious gratitude that they had done all in their power to come to his rescue when he needed it. But they noted too that recent events, while they might have tempered his pride, did not seem to have shattered his self-confidence. Within a few hours of their arrival he was putting forward plans for the future.

After a great deal of discussion and planning, it was agreed that William's son William would trade under the name of William Hay (junior) and Company, together with his brother Charles. When their father was discharged from bankruptcy he would join them in the business. Their aim would be to re-open markets for salted fish, beginning by acting as agents for other merchants. William was also very lucky to have influential and wealthy friends and relatives who would no doubt in due course lend him money to set up in business again. One of the very first people to offer assistance, was Henry Cheyne, William's son-in-law, and a well-off lawyer in Edinburgh. He appointed William junior factor for his lands in Shetland, and early in March 1843 came up for a visit with Barbara his wife and their three young sons.

William enjoyed his grandsons' boisterous company and seeing his beloved daughter again. Henry Cheyne had business to attend to in Tangwick, but they stayed long enough in Lerwick for him to discuss with William and his sons how they were going to carry on trade without enough boats.

Meals in the Hay household were much soberer affairs these days and there was no longer wine to drink. The four men, William, tense and grey, but whose shoulders were still upright, Henry Cheyne, tall and lithe with smooth jet black hair and very even features, William and Charles, very alike with lank fair hair and the large Ogilvy nose and jaw, sat round the table together when the meal was over. At each end a candle shone steadily, lighting up their features and placing the corners of the room in shadow.

"The fish trade has been decimated", began William senior. "The men have no boats and no equipment."

"What we need is more boats to hire out," said Charles, waving his hand and making the candle flicker.

"We haven't the capital to do it," said William junior. "We must be realistic. We're trading strictly for cash and the banks won't lend us a penny."

"I think the only way we can succeed is to get the fish to market before anyone else," insisted William senior. "I've learnt that over the years. And we need to find new outlets."

Up till now Henry Cheyne had said nothing. He was sizing up what each of them was saying and trying, as an outsider, to conclude what would be the best course. Now he spoke.

"I'm willing to lend you money," he said in measured tones. "I've been wondering the best way to do it. I'm prepared to forward the capital to buy, shall we say, eight small boats? We can work out a scheme whereby you repay me when times are better."

"That's a very generous offer," said William senior, his voice full of gratitude. "And it's just what we needed. Thank you Henry. You don't know how much this means to us."

When William told his wife of Henry's offer she could see hope rekindled in his eyes.

"Thank God you have such a supportive family," she said, "to come to your help in this crisis."

"I couldn't get through without them. Without you in particular," he said, kissing her on the forehead. "I know I've been difficult to live with lately." He looked at his wife's pale face and large dark eyes. She looked very fragile.

"Things will work out," she said softly. "You'll see."

He kissed her gently again.

"Let's hope so," he said.

(2)

By summer William Hay junior had a small fleet of sloops fishing for cod and was sending off the salted fish to Dublin, Bilbao and beyond. One day William senior called on his son to see how things were going. His son passed him an invoice that had come from an English agent in St Petersburg.

"What's this?" asked William. "Russia?"

"I thought it worth a try," replied his son. "And we must see if we can't recapture some of the West Indian market."

"That's really been dead since the Slave Trade was abolished," said his father. "Now they no longer feed the slaves on salted fish, the market's collapsed. But I think your policy is sound. Oh, if only I wasn't prevented from trading myself. It is so frustrating to have to leave it all to you. I remember when I first worked with your grandfather. He was always so full of ideas, I sometimes had to draw the line."

"Well, they can't stop you airing your ideas," said William junior. "You were still very young when you came back to Shetland to live," he continued. "Charles and I have had a bit of time to see the world. And presumably, when you get on your feet..." He paused.

William senior thought back wistfully to the great plans he'd had for his eldest son James, whose own ideas on life had cut short any thought of a father-son partnership even before his tragic death had taken him away for good. William knew now that you couldn't fashion your children according to your own wishes, but had to leave them free. And being left free to choose William and Charles had both decided to come home when he needed it. He wasn't going to jeopardise this warm relationship by insisting they stay longer than they wanted.

"We'll take things as they come," he said generously.

(3)

A few days after this conversation, William found himself entering the huge and imposing gateway into Fort Charlotte on his way to the courthouse. It was twelve o'clock and the sun shone quite high in the sky on the bare green island lying low on the other side of the harbour. He idly watched the enormous herring gulls with their yellow beaks perched on the walls of the fort, or on the cannon still standing in the embrasures. The little town of Lerwick, all grey stone with slate roofs, lay peacefully below. One or two ships were hove to in the harbour. It was a pleasant summer day, to be savoured and enjoyed, yet William felt far from happy.

In his pocket he carried a summons, "for the examination of William Hay the Bankrupt", in connection with a bond that had been granted by two of his sons in favour of his brother Andrew. He had been requested to furnish books, private letters and other correspondence which he had previously failed to submit, to the trustees of Hay and Ogilvy's estate. It was the expression, "William Hay the Bankrupt" that stuck in his throat. Even if his sons had rallied round and had started the business again, he was still some kind of social outcast to be treated differently from other people. His face burned with shame as he approached the low white buildings inside the fort now used as a temporary courthouse. It didn't matter that he had friends among the lairds who had planned or were planning to offer loans to restore his credit. His son-in-law Andrew Humphrey, Anne's husband, John Bruce the laird from Sumburgh, Dr Edmonston's brother in the island of Unst, they had all proffered their support. But it didn't make any difference.

The sheriff's officer was curt and not impressed by the letters he produced from Henry Cheyne in Edinburgh, correspondents in Liverpool and a number from his son Andrew in Calcutta. It seemed that the only thing that brought you respect in this world was money, and money, he had discovered recently, was not necessarily what made you happy. It was people that counted more than anything, the comfort of his wife, the joy of his grandchildren, the support of his relatives and friends. It was only when they were all you had left, that you realised just how much they meant to you. Nevertheless they didn't understand the humiliation he felt at being dragged before a court to explain some of his financial dealings. He had to put on as brave a face as he could to the onlookers, and hope that his discharge would come soon.

(4)

Meanwhile Charles Ogilvy had set up another business with his sons, in competition with William Hay and Company. From the trustees of Hay and Ogilvy's, they obtained the lease of all the premises at Freefield, and Blackness at Scalloway and secured the right to dispose of all the fish of the Isles of Burra. Of the two rival companies, it looked at first very much as if Charles Ogilvy and Company was more likely to succeed.

In July 1843 Charles got his discharge. William, however, would have to wait. Relations between the families were still cool, and here was another source of bitterness between them.

One day a few weeks after he had learnt the news, William was walking in Lerwick and chanced on Barbara Ogilvy and her two teenage children Jane and Charles, outside the circulating library. Barbara was the widow of Charles' brother John, who had died three years previously at West Sandwick in Yell, and they were staying with the Ogilvys at Seafield.

William and Barbara knew each other well, and after exchanging a few remarks of a general nature, Barbara said to William suddenly," William, can't you and Charles make it up? It's ages since we've seen you at Seafield."

William's lips tightened. "We've nothing to say to one another," he said tersely. "We've gone our separate ways."

"Surely that's now over and done with?" persisted Barbara, still an attractive widow of thirty-five with auburn hair and green eyes. "You're still in . business together..."

"Charles may be back in business, but I'm still forbidden to trade," said William and there was real bitterness in his voice. "It's simply not fair. How do you think I feel having to watch my sons doing my job?"

Barbara tried another tack. "Charles is a changed man," she said quietly. "This has all been a bitter blow to him too. Can't you accept that, not even for your wife's sake?"

William hesitated for a moment. Dragging his dead wife into the matter wasn't fair. He now regretted the scene he had made last year when he had confronted Charles. He should have taken steps to put things right between them. Now months had passed by and the rift had grown deeper. It would require a great loss of face on William's part to put himself in the wrong and ask for Charles' forgiveness.

"I've told you, it's no use," he said in an irritated tone. "I'm sorry, Barbara. The past's over and done with. We've got our own lives to lead."

He took his leave of Barbara and the children and walked away, but with a heavy heart, because he felt things could have been very different, and because in the little world of Lerwick society, where everyone was inter-related, or at least knew everyone else, it was difficult to avoid meeting each other from time to time.

(5)

As the autumn came on and chilly winds began to blow and all-pervading mists rolled in from the sea, Margaret Hay took a turn for the worse. Her eyes were bright, her skin very pale and she developed a dry little cough which persisted and left her exhausted. William called in old Doctor Spence who examined her and came downstairs to see William without a smile.

"I'm afraid it's bad news," he said to William who grew alarmed at the expression on his face. "Consumption. There's not a lot to be done. Give her

117

plenty of good food, plenty of fresh air and keep her warm. Maybe with attention and rest..."

His voice tried to sound reassuring but trailed off into silence.

When the doctor had gone William sank into a chair and buried his face in his hands. He remembered how radiant his wife had looked when he had courted her in Glasgow, how willing she had been to come up to live with him in Shetland. She had taken on the duties of wife and mother to his children with eagerness and immediately got on good terms with her stepchildren. She had borne him little Meg, who was more like a granddaughter to him and the source of much joy.

But as soon as she had come north, business had gone from bad to worse, nothing had gone right and she had seen the firm collapse, William lose his position and be declared bankrupt. They had lost all their property, even the home he had brought her to at Hayfield, where she had lived in comfort. Then she had lost a child, and if that hadn't been enough, they had been forced to move and reduce their style of living. Little wonder she was ill.

But that dreaded word "consumption", the illness for which there was no known cure, that was something different. Would it take her away from him altogether? He groaned. He thought of his bursts of sudden moodiness and bad temper of recent months, his aloofness, his lack of concern. She had never lost faith in him. But how was he to conceal the truth from her in the days to come, to pretend that things were still the same? Every day seemed to present him with a new challenge. He made up his mind. She mustn't know. Nor must the children.

"We must keep you warm day and night," he said, almost too brightly when he went upstairs again. "And you are to do as little as possible. We'll soon have you as right as rain."

He had the feeling that she herself suspected what he already knew, but she said nothing. They were both people of courage who respected each other's right to silence.

But as the winter drew on, a shadow hung over the household.

(6)

During all this time William was not idle. He wrote dozens of letters to contacts in Scotland and England against the time when he would be able to resume trading. He sat in his little study, quill pen in hand, his fingers stained with ink, exploring as many outlets as possible, trying all the while to sound positive.

"When I had the pleasure of meeting you on board the steamer in the summer of 1842, I was not aware that you had engaged in plaice fishing," he wrote, his ill-cut pen scratching the paper as the clock ticked away steadily in the corner of the room.

"You will no doubt have heard of the stoppage of our House."

"It gives me much pleasure to hear lately from a sometime friend of your son in Newcastle."

Each boat going south took a bundle of mail, each letter carefully composed and handwritten.

In December William revisited the mainland to re-establish contacts with suppliers and agents and to order stock to build up a new retail store. Among those he called on was Thomas Worthington in Manchester, whose father had been a friend of James Hay. Thomas had a factory that wove silk and cotton ribbons, cotton tapes and thread, not far from the Market Place. It was not the first time that William had been there, but on this occasion Manchester seemed an even busier place than before, with squares and streets filling with impressive new homes, replacing the old wood-and-plaster houses which still remained in odd corners. In the neighbourhoods surrounding the great cotton-spinning and calico-printing works, huge numbers of poor cheapjack housing was going up, to give homes to the hordes of factory workers pouring into the town from the countryside.

On the first evening of his arrival, Thomas and William sat down together after a meal to smoke pipes and discuss how William was to start out again in business. Thomas proposed to loan him the tidy sum of one thousand pounds, to acquire premises in Lerwick and to buy stock.

"I should concentrate to begin with on setting up a retail outlet," said Thomas reflectively, pulling on his pipe. "You have a wide circle of contacts. And if you provide items needed every day by people in Shetland, or by the whaling crews, you can't go wrong."

"Times are very hard," said William doubtfully. "No one has any money. There are more people destitute than I ever remember."

"But wealth generates wealth," said Thomas. "That's our philosophy down here. Once you get started things will start to snowball. And you say William and Charles are already making some headway in the fish trade."

"When I think how well we were doing twelve years ago," said William with feeling. "Before the great hurricane."

"Just as well we don't know what's going to happen in life," said Thomas. "Maybe we shouldn't have the courage to face it. Now, tomorrow I want to take you to see someone who knows how to grasp fate by the throat. Thomas Potter deals in textiles, Lancashire cottons and fustians, Yorkshire linens and flannels, and now he's moved to George Street he's gone into silk ribbons, hosiery and haberdashery. I should think his must be the largest and most influential establishment here in Manchester."

When next day they reached Thomas Potter's warehouse; William was amazed at what he saw. It was six storeys high, with a wide frontage. To raise the great quantities of cotton and woollen goods that arrived at the warehouse in horse-drawn vans, steam hoists were being used: a very modern invention. fifty workmen were employed in the warehouse, packing and unpacking the bales. William was fascinated to see that great care was being taken to see that each bale was packed according to its destination – bales intended for China packed in the Chinese manner and decorated with little pictures representing Chinese customs and ceremonies. Great thought was also being given as to how the goods were later to be transported, on the backs of elephants or camels or by sea.

In the main office Thomas and William met Thomas Potter himself. William was introduced as a visitor from Shetland shortly to start up in business there.

"I must give you a copy of my catalogue," said Thomas Potter brightly, a short ginger-haired, restless man of obvious intelligence and drive.

William murmured admiration for all he saw going on about him.

"Well, we started from very small beginnings," said Thomas rather modestly for someone so successful. "Hard work, luck, and being in the right place at the right time. Now you see, most merchants wanted to stay down near the Market Place. I've taken the risk and moved out here, and it's already beginning to pay off. Now, if you'll excuse me, I have an important order to attend to."

And he bustled off, leaving William and Thomas Worthington to continue their tour.

William was heartened by what he saw down in Manchester. Business was obviously thriving, and he met several other entrepreneurs besides Thomas Potter who inspired him with confidence and enthusiasm.

When finally he returned to Lerwick, he felt refreshed and ready to begin all over again.

(7)

William's optimism continued when on the 1st January, 1844, he obtained his discharge. He acquired a house, wharf and warehouse at the end of the beach with a small office attached to it, and was lucky through friends in Edinburgh to engage the services of Peter Ross, a young schoolteacher from Scotland who was willing to leave a poorly-paid post in the capital and venture up to Shetland to become his clerk. On the other side of the street William rented a shop, and planned to set himself up as a general merchant. Besides Peter he had only two people to help him, a shop assistant and a warehouse-keeper.

Peter was in his early twenties, short, dark and intense, more used to dealing with unruly youngsters than with business. He hadn't the temperament for imposing his will on boys unwilling to learn, and had eagerly agreed to try the work of a merchant's clerk. He had a good head for figures, and was intelligent, but he'd had absolutely no training. He had also come up to Shetland looking upon it as some kind of adventure, quite unprepared for the amount of hard work there would be to get a new business off the ground, and little suspecting the dreariness of the long winter days ahead of him. William would have to teach him everything. But it was enough in the beginning for William to be free to work again, and in fact the idea of starting everything from scratch rather appealed to him. William junior and his brother Charles were still a great support, and after the first few months William felt himself back in his stride.

In the spring he rode down the coast over treacherous paths to see John Bruce at Sandlodge. Chilly winds blew in from the sea but a gentle sunlight played over the rugged cliffs and the sea in the distance, and over the low outline of the island of Mousa. It was very peaceful down below by the little bay and as he rode up to the gates of the mansion; he had many memories of coming there as a boy with his father. Then it had been the present laird's father he had come to see. This John Bruce was some eleven years younger than William, still in the prime of life, and had served for some years in the Navy before becoming Deputy Lieutenant for Shetland. William was beholden to John because he had been sympathetic when Hay and Ogilvy's had failed, and offered him a loan to help him re-establish himself. Like William he was a family man, having had thirteen children, and as they sat drinking in the large drawing room with its views out over the sea, they had plenty of news to exchange.

"As you know I've been very fortunate," said William. "William and Charles have given me every support. Though I think Charles is getting restless: as you know his wife Jessica was born in Jamaica and finds the climate here very difficult. And they want to get the boys settled into schools in Edinburgh."

"And your wife?" pursued John Bruce.

William sighed. "Not good," he said briefly. "I suppose you've guessed it's consumption. We live for the moment."

"You ought to try to get her away to a warmer climate," said John. "At least for the winter. Away from our rains and gales and endless mists."

"That's not easy at the moment," said William. "I'm hardly back on my feet yet. Now, what was the proposition you had to put to me?"

"Well, I've decided to give up handling the fish cured on our beaches in the east of the south mainland," began John. "And my cousin at Bigton on the west coast wants to do the same. I'm involved in so many matters and away such a lot of the time that I for one would like to see the whole of this area handed over to someone else. With all your experience and knowledge of dealing with fish in this region, you seem the obvious choice. What do you say?"

William took a deep breath. This was an opening he had not expected. It would consolidate his hold on the ling fishing over the whole of the south of Shetland.

"I'd like to hear more," he said enthusiastically.

"Well, if you've got the courage to trust the fishing again there is profit to be made," went on John. "Merchants are more and more taking over the fishing from the landlords. The old ways of life are changing. And I'd be glad to do you a favour."

"I know you prefer to cure the fish yourselves," he went on. "But the fishermen have always salted their own fish and sold them in the dried state. If you can supply them with salt, I think you can do a deal with them."

"Our sloop *Albion* can run up salt from Liverpool," said William, "and unload it all round the coast. That's no problem."

Before William left they went on to discuss finance and other necessary arrangements.

"This is good news," William told his sons when he returned. "It's a step in the right direction."

(8)

In May, to William's surprise, his application to take over Freefield and the installations at Blacksness at Scalloway for three years was also granted. He and his son William went down to Freefield for the first time in nearly two years. It was a strange moment as he strode round the quays with his son, re-renting the property he had once called his own. He thought of his son James' death and of his own bankruptcy. It made him feel the fragility of human affairs and the folly of believing anything could be permanent. There were still fishing boats tied up along the quayside, but the roofs in the curing shed, the shipbuilding yard and the carpenters' workshop were in a bad state of repair. William could have wept to see the state of the place. The flitboats used for unloading the larger vessels were falling to pieces and there was no sign of the busy hum of activity that had once filled the place.

"Repair the boats, mend the roofs, repaint the office, get the place started again." William mentally made notes. "Charles Ogilvy seems to have done nothing here. We shall have our hands full."

"We can move the books back into the office," said William junior, who shared his father's dynamic approach to life. "If you like I can see to that tomorrow. And Charles can engage some carpenters – how many do you think we can afford? There are dozens of unemployed men ready to jump at the offer of a job."

"Can we ever get things back to where they were?" asked William wistfully, half to himself.

"We can have a good try," said his son wholeheartedly.

Once he regained Blacksness, from which to re-launch the cod-fishing from Scalloway, William set up another little shop there. His friend Thomas Worthington, who saw retailing as a key part of his business, had fired him with enthusiasm. The young man appointed in charge of the store was Jeremiah Malcolmson, a local resident of Scalloway, a sandy-haired, likeable character with a lot of drive. He got on well with William and looked set to get on well with local people, who came in to buy the tea, coffee, whisky, brandy and even tobacco, along with everyday goods, they needed. Although a cart track ran up the Tingwall Valley, there was no proper road to Scalloway, and both men and women had to bring all the goods carried in large baskets on their backs. Where possible everything went by sea, but it was a long and hazardous journey from Lerwick to Scalloway round by Sumburgh Head. This naturally increased the price of imported goods for the local community.

But it was a bad time for William to be starting up in business again. The first season's cod and herring fishing was disappointing and life was still hard for most of the population. They had little money to spare to spend in William's shops and the future did not look good. Again the crops failed.

Later that spring William and Charles came to their father looking very serious.

"It's no use," began Charles. "There's not a living here for all of us."

"But things must pick up soon," said William hopefully, though his heart sank. He guessed what they were about to say.

"Father, we've made up our minds," I'm sorry," said William junior. "You know we didn't intend to stay for long."

"We've just got to think of ourselves and our own futures," added Charles.

"We've both fixed up jobs in banks in Edinburgh, "said William junior. "We're leaving at the end of May."

This was a huge blow to William. Little glimmers of hope had appeared on the horizon and it had helped immensely having Charles and William there to lean on. Now, in adverse circumstances, he was going to have to work harder than at any time in his life. As he reluctantly accepted that his sons had the right to choose what was best for themselves, for him the future looked bleak. At fifty-six, with everything against him, he must struggle on alone.

CHAPTER ELEVEN

Struggles

William seemed saddened by the departure of his sons. Here he was engaged in rebuilding the family firm, and yet William and Charles had returned to Edinburgh, and Andrew and John had settled out in Calcutta and were unlikely to return. Neither William's sister nor his brothers had produced heirs who would want to join him in business, except James who was far away in New York. And who would leave America for Shetland where prospects were so unpromising?

That left George, just finishing his education at school in Montrose. With all the turmoil of the last two years little had been said about his future. William had wondered if he too would go out to India like his brother John at the age of sixteen. But now the obvious solution was for George to come home and work with him in Lerwick. Whatever dreams George had of going to India, or of joining Charles in Edinburgh, would have to be dashed, just as his own hopes had been shattered when he had had to leave Aberdeen and come back to Lerwick to help his father. Family ties counted most, and young men were supposed to obey their fathers. There was an inexorable fate at work here.

George had suffered deeply from the death of his own mother and Margaret Scott had tried to be especially kind to him because when she had married William he had been at an awkward age poised between boyhood and manhood, when boys were ultra-sensitive and hid their feelings beneath an aggressive manner. William realised with guilt that apart from little Meg he had not had much time or concern for George or his other younger children, Thomas, Arthur and Mary. They had all suffered from William's bankruptcy, having to move their home and change their life-style and grow up in a world which now offered them less security and hopes for the future. William had no real idea what George's reaction would be. He decided to write to him at school in Montrose to broach the matter and discuss things more fully when he arrived home.

George was of medium height, with thin brown straight hair and an honest face. Over the past few months he had been away he seemed to have matured and greeted his father at first with reserve and then with sudden warmth. There was no sign of any grudge in his attitude as if his father had shattered some cherished dream, and William suddenly wondered if his son hadn't taken his suggestion rather as a compliment and an opportunity. When they sat down together to talk, he picked his words carefully, talking about the business, stressing the positive advances they had made, treating him almost like an equal.

"I miss your brothers," he went on. "They've been a great deal of help and support. Just now I've been wondering what I'm going to do. Have you considered the letter I sent you recently?"

George raised candid eyes to his father and spoke not like a callow boy but like someone who had digested and considered the implications of what he is about to say.

"You want me to stay at home and learn the business," he said. "Work with you to build it up."

William nodded.

"I realise it's a risky occupation," he said, and his knuckles on the table were tense. "I can't guarantee we shall succeed. After all we've been through these last two years."

"I've always been interested," said George unexpectedly. "Only you never seemed to have time to explain things before."

"That's something I regret," said William ruefully. "But now I'm talking seriously. We'll work together and I'll try to teach you all I know. I'll take you into partnership. And if things don't work out, then I'll give you the freedom to seek your fortune elsewhere."

He paused and watched anxiously to see the effect of this little speech on George. At the word "partnership" the boys' eyes looked eager.

"I never thought it would be left to me," he said a little breathlessly. "Father, it's what I always wanted to do."

William shaded his eyes with his hand, to conceal the sudden emotion he felt at his son's answer.

"George I'm so glad," he said, thrusting his arm round George's shoulder. "William Hay and Son. And we're going to succeed."

(2)

But business did not promise well at first. William could not leave a boy barely sixteen at attend to matters William and Charles had handled with ease, and he soon realised he could not expect him to oversee financial affairs. Although George had been a promising scholar, William was amazed at the gaps in his general knowledge and his unawareness of the ways of the world. Sometimes he was over-anxious, sometimes naive, sometimes he made mistakes which

126

William had not foreseen. His father gradually became aware what a trial he himself must have been to James or even to Mr Fryer at the outset of his apprenticeship. As a young person you could never see a parent's point of view, and by the time you grew up to understand them, it was too late. And what a wealth of patience and understanding you needed to guide the young! William was sometimes exasperated and frustrated but he did all he could to control his temper. From working with his father George gained a pride and an emotional security he had never known before.

Poor prospects made William's clerk Peter Ross realise that there was little future for him in Lerwick. He was not one of those people who came to Shetland and fell in love with the island and its people, and discovered a way of life to which they could adapt. He had spent all his life in Edinburgh, and after the initial novelty of a place so different from his home, began to long for the wider horizons and greater excitement of the capital. William had not found him easy to get on with, as he was subject to moodiness and was too proud to accept advice or criticism. William had done all he could to encourage him, but by the end of May Peter had made up his mind to leave. This left William in a spot with only his son George to help him, and for a while it looked as if the business could founder all over again.

He had added cause for concern over his wife's health. Margaret Hay had had a bad winter, and William finally agreed she should go south to Edinburgh and spend the summer with her brother at Rothesay. Seeing no alternative, he left George to try to cope with any urgent matters, till his return, and went south with her. He stayed only one night, and then began the tedious journey back to Shetland, torn between concern for his wife and worry over his business. George was growing up rapidly, but to leave him entirely in charge was too great a burden to lay on the young man's shoulders.

At first William received encouraging letters. The better weather was doing Margaret good, she was able to take little outings, her appetite had revived and she was seeing old friends. In Lerwick the house seemed strangely empty without her, and William began to hope that perhaps after a time she would come back and rejoin him. Then came the news that she was not doing so well, and was going to see a specialist. His considered verdict was that Margaret should not spend another winter in Shetland. With business precarious and four younger children besides George to care for, William wondered agonisingly what he was going to do.

For a while he considered the possibility of abandoning his business in Shetland and of going to take a paid post somewhere abroad, where his wife could join him, somewhere with a warmer climate, where she could endure the winter months. The place he most favoured was Guernsey, near enough to France to enjoy a mild winter, but where English was spoken and English ways understood. The thought sustained him over several weeks while he wrote letters and made enquiries, but times were bad and every reply was negative. He resigned himself to being separated from his wife, and struggled on under great pressure. Lines appeared on his forehead, and a tense and weary look filled his eyes. He seemed to have entered a long black tunnel with scarcely a chink of the light of hope at the end of it.

(3)

"Haven't you heard the news?"

William was passing down Lerwick's main street on the way to his warehouse.

"What news?"

It was a merchant from the other end of town who had approached him; a big, hearty, insensitive sort of man William had never really liked.

"Charles Ogilvy, collapsed and died. Had a heart attack or something. Only a short while ago."

The brutal announcement of his brother-in-law's death shocked William. He somehow felt that as a relative he should have heard the news at first hand from the Ogilvys themselves. It was June and a pleasant sunny morning with the sea calm and the gulls screeching overhead. Several months had passed since he had seen Charles and even when they had been forced to meet, William had insisted on remaining cool and aloof. Charles was only forty-two and William had not foreseen that he might die, and that the possibility for reconciliation might be gone forever. A wave of regret swept over him. Why had he been so obstinate? Why had he given way to pride? He and Charles had worked together for years, and however bitter their differences over the failure of Hay and Ogilvy's, he should not have allowed his feelings to overcome ties of family and friendship.

"I hadn't heard," he said briefly. "I'd better go and see what I can do."

The man looked at William curiously. It was common knowledge that Charles and William were no longer on speaking terms and that there was a rift between their families. Too late he realised that perhaps he should not have interfered in a private grief, and stood there helplessly as William turned and set off to go home.

On returning William went into his study and shut the door. What could he do now? Go to Martha, Charles' wife, and ask for her forgiveness? Try to explain to Barbara why he had acted as he did? Was this the moment to intrude on their grief?

He ran his hands helplessly through his hair.

If only he had said something, last week, yesterday! Now it was too late. He took out a quill pen and paper and began several times without success to write a letter of condolences. When finally he was satisfied he sealed it in an envelope and went down to the warehouse to tell George that he was going over to Seafield. Once again he would have to leave George to manage a newly arrived consignment of timber from Hamburg on his own.

He strode along to Sound on foot, feeling as guilty as a conspirator does.

The servant girl was surprised to see him, and said discreetly that she didn't know if Mrs Ogilvy was available. She took the letter and went off, leaving William in the cool and deserted hall, where he had so often been received with affection.

After a while there was a movement on the stairs. Martha Ogilvy appeared above him, in black, stern yet dignified in her grief.

"I'm surprised you had the nerve to come here after your recent behaviour," she said in a tense low voice. "I've read your letter. You say you regret what has happened. Charles never got over the failure of the firm, and the way you treated him has hastened his death, of that I'm sure. He was talking of you only yesterday. It's too late to tell him you are sorry. He died thinking you hated him. There's nothing more I can say. You have only yourself to blame."

William said nothing. Martha turned and went slowly back up the stairs. He stumbled to the door and down the steps, shoulders bent and head lowered, sick with remorse.

(4)

Shortly after Charles' Ogilvy's death, the firm of Charles Ogilvy and Company foundered. William ruefully reflected that in a competitive world one man's failure meant another man's success and that with his rival out of the field he might have more chance to succeed.

Another sign of hope was when he was appointed by the Earl of Zetland to be factor of all his estate, which meant, together with the fishing, that he would be running a considerable part of Mainland.

There were wide responsibilities which included seeing to the day to day duties of the estate, visiting the tenants to listen to their grievances, settling disputes that arose among them and collecting their rents. It all brought him into closer contact with the lives of the crofters. While he had always respected the fishermen he met at the fishing stations for the tough lives they led and the dangers they faced at sea, now he met them at home in their crofts, with their wives and families. In these difficult times when some men were still unable to go to sea, some families couldn't pay their rents and but for the compassion of the landlords would be evicted. William, who when faced with bankruptcy had felt he had lost all he had striven for, on seeing the abject poverty of some of these people's lives, was humbled and full of admiration for their courage and endurance. He realised that in comparison with them he was still rich and this thought did much to sustain his spirits when he was tempted to lose heart. He discovered how grateful these poor people were when he simply took the trouble to give them some of his time, to show an interest in their problems and do what little he could for them. This was totally different from the way he had treated his tenants at Laxfirth and he discovered that their genuine gratitude meant a lot to him.

Not only were there families where children had died young, there was one crofter who had lost a son the same age as William's son James. Talking to the man about his loss made William realise that he had never been able to express his own grief before. And this common loss created a bond between them that had nothing to do with class or position in life.

William had also to see to the upkeep of churches and manses on the estate, deal with the payment of ministers' stipends, and visit them on a regular basis. Over the last few years Methodist preachers and Quakers had visited Lerwick, and William like many others had gone to their meetings. There were deep rifts in the Church of Scotland, and a lot of controversy about church practices. The ministers found William a willing listener.

He rode down one day to visit the minister at Bigton, where the manse was perched on a windy hillside overlooking the sea. Sheep grazed right up to the minister's door.

The minister Mr Farley was a big hearty red-faced man who practised temperance and entertained William with tea. William had been telling him about the other people he had to visit in Bigton.

"I've first to see Thomas Mallinson the schoolmaster about some repairs at the school," he said," and call upon the overseer about the poor rates."

"You're a very busy man," said the minister.

"I can't always even get to the kirk on Sunday," said William, a little guiltily. "The boat comes in from Leith on Sundays and there's so much to do."

"The Lord made the Sabbath holy to give us rest each week," said Mr Farley somewhat sternly. "You can't overwork your body and go without sleep and you shouldn't overwork your soul. Don't you ever take a break?"

"I had eighteen months of enforced idleness when I was bankrupt," said William. "But my daughter Anne and her three youngsters are coming to see me next month from Reawick, and I shall take time off then."

"God has blessed you with a large family," said Mr Farley. "Well, I'll see the leak in the roof's mended. We'll have another talk when you are here again."

And he waved from his gate as William rode down the stony path to the huddle of crofts by the sea.

(5)

In August Anne and her children came to stay. The had a tiring wet journey from Reawick with porters carrying their luggage and the young mother trying to cope with three children under four.

All her young days and adolescence Anne had lived at Hayfield, and in her exhaustion she openly criticised the reduction in size and facilities of the house where William was living.

William, who had been looking forward to her visit, especially with his wife away in Scotland, hugged his fractious daughter and tried to help her settle the children. Anne's husband was also away in Scotland, and she found life empty and boring in Reawick. But she hadn't quite realised what staying with William in straitened circumstances might mean.

"I don't like this place, Father," she said rather like a spoilt child, on her first evening. "Will you have to stay here long?"

"It was the best solution at the time." said William, as he, George, Arthur and Meg sat with Anne round the table. "Anne, you have to realise that things have changed. And we don't do so badly. Only we don't entertain as we used to. You'll have to get used to it."

Anne had looked forward to coming to Lerwick to see a little more society, to visit old friends who like her were married and catch up with gossip. The next morning she put on a fashionable dress and went to call on a young woman who still lived in Lerwick. William's little daughter and Anne's children were being looked after by a friend, and refreshed by a good night's sleep she set off in high spirits. William and George had business to attend to, but on returning to the house at mid-day George found his elder sister in floods of tears.

"Maria was scarcely polite," she said petulantly. "She made it clear she didn't want to see me and had plenty of other friends. Then she said, in a very rude way, that she had to go out, and when I asked her if she would call on me, she seemed embarrassed and said it wasn't the same as when we lived at Hayfield."

"It's happened to me too," said George quietly. "Come Anne, don't be upset. It's because Father went bankrupt. Some people are snobs and they only want to mix with people who are well off and successful. They don't want to

131

have to talk about bankruptcies and the like. They only want to see Uncle Andrew because he's rich. It makes me sick."

Anne looked at her brother in surprise through her tears and sat down. Although George was now as tall as she was, she had not realised that he had grown up.

"We shall be rich and successful again, you'll see," he went on, with the overweening optimism of youth. "Father's taken me into partnership."

"I hadn't realised things had been so bad," said Anne, drying her face. "I was so rude last night. Father didn't explain."

"I think life's very difficult for him," said George, with an insight beyond his years. "With our stepmother ill and away."

"Do you really get on with her?" asked Anne.

"She's been very kind to me. What's going to happen, Anne? Will she die?"

"I don't know," said Anne. "Has father said anything?"

"It's consumption, I know," said George. "He hasn't told us but I can tell by his face. Anne, do be kind to him."

Anne said little to her father about her visit to her friend but William realised from her changed attitude that something had happened. He was convinced she had been slighted on his account and it made him angry.

For once he tried to put business out of mind and enjoy the company of his family. But it wasn't easy to forget his worries for long.

(6)

In September a letter came from the Scott family to say that Margaret's specialist recommended she spend the winter in Madeira. Her sister agreed to go with her. Once again William went south leaving George in charge and accompanied the two women by boat down to Southampton. It was a very fraught trip. William had not seen his wife for several months and was aghast to see how she had altered. In the cramped conditions of the ship, with her sister always at hand, it was difficult to be alone together. Margaret asked about the children, especially about Meg, but her life had been spent for six months in Scotland and now with all the excitement and stress of going to Madeira, he felt they were moving apart. And who knew if she would ever come back again?

He went with them aboard the ship lying moored in Southampton harbour and saw where they would spend the nine days of the voyage. Conditions were not ideal for a sick woman and he fussed over her, unable to express his real feelings. She clung to him and said goodbye as if she too wondered whether they would ever see each other again. He couldn't forget her pale face as he went ashore and watched the ship leave on the high tide.

On the way back he caught a ship up the east coast that called in at Hull. It was some years now since he had been there and after they had berthed in the dock he decided to spend some time revisiting the town. The place was even more bustling than he remembered it. Another dock had been constructed and many new houses had been built to replace the old timber-framed dwellings. He lingered in the High Street walking past Mr Fryer's old business, now called Robert Fryer and Sons, half expecting to see Paul or Peter or even Mr Fryer come down the steps to greet him. After a drink at the King's Head which didn't seem to have changed much, he wandered on in a reverie, thinking of the times when he had lived there, even recalling his jealousy of his brother Andrew. It made him smile to think he had ever been jealous of Andrew.

Finally almost without noticing it, he found himself in front of the local school. As he stood there, suddenly the faces of boys he had forgotten for years flashed into his mind. They were still young, still fresh, and still hopeful, they hadn't changed in his memory. But in fact of course, they must all be as old as he was, some dead, some would have children, some even grandchildren in school now. There was a conflict in his mind between the powerful memory and the present reality. Then a bright-eyed schoolboy came out, in modern dress. The memory was shattered.

He moved on.

Next high tide they sailed for Leith. Although he was anxious to get back to Shetland, he stopped in Edinburgh to see Peter Scott and give him news of his sisters' departure.

When he finally reached Lerwick he hastened home to find all well with George, Arthur and Meg. Nothing untoward had happened during his absence. But an immense backlog of work had piled up. It was the time of the year when the fishermen from both east and west coasts of the mainland came to him in Lerwick to be paid for the sale of their fish. He had left it much later than usual and the men were clamouring for their money. They besieged his door in groups of a dozen or more and he had to sit down to the accounts each evening in addition to all the other tasks required of him. Since Peter Ross had left he had no clerk, and there was no one who could help him. Night after night he sat up till long after midnight working by candlelight with a determination that few that had not known him as a child could appreciate. He was working far harder than he had ever worked in Hull. He didn't heed Mr Farley's advice that he needed regular rest. He flogged himself mercilessly, single-mindedly. He would not be beaten.

CHAPTER TWELVE

Fighting Back

The year 1845 started well for William. He gradually began to recover some of his property. Through a friend, Thomas Edmonston of Unst, he regained Hayfield and extensive lands in the Tingwall Valley. It was a red-letter day when he and his family moved back into Hayfield. Even George was delighted and little Arthur ran into every corner to see what had changed. William too savoured every moment and wrote enthusiastically to Thomas at school in Montrose and to Mary in Aberdeen, telling them that when they next returned to Shetland they would be coming "home". Other servants were engaged, and although times were not what they were, there was a greater sense of comfort and security. William's hard work had begun to pay off. George too had done his best, and was pulling his weight. Hay and Son was beginning to feel its way and to make profits. Being granted back the lease of the isles of Burra extended their control of the fishery.

Early in the year Thomas Worthington, William's Manchester friend, had offered him another loan to buy back a schooner that had belonged to Hay and Ogilvy's but had been sold like so much other property when the firm failed. She was called the *Janet Hay* after the little daughter William had loved and lost so young. He vividly remembered the day five years earlier when the ship was completed at Freefield, and launched into the harbour there, a great achievement for the yard and the scene of much rejoicing on the part of workmen and friends. Now it was just what they needed, a proper cargo vessel, capable of taking on twenty-two hands, and travelling a considerable distance. Freefield was thriving once again and fitting out Hay and Son's vessels as well as repairing many other boats that called there.

When the simmer dim returned to Shetland at the beginning of June, Margaret Hay came back from Madeira. She seemed happy to live at Hayfield again and her pale cheeks had recovered a little hectic colour. The children were delighted to see her and William was pleased that she was able to ride out each day in a carriage to take the air. The weather was warm and sunny and for a few brief weeks family life was almost back to normal. But William knew that those precious moments would not last, and that his wife hadn't long to live.

(2)

One morning when William was sitting in his study writing letters the door suddenly burst open and there stood three-year-old little Meg. She would normally have earned a reprimand for disturbing him at his work, but seeing the look of terror on the child's face he sensed immediately that this was no ordinary occasion.

"Why Meg, what's the matter?" he asked in alarm.

"It's Mother, she won't answer me, "said the child. "She won't move. Come quickly."

William's heart sank. He flung down his quill pen and rushed into the drawing room. His wife Margaret who liked to sit downstairs for part of each day, was sitting on the couch, her head slumped on her chest. He could see at once that she was dead. He stared unbelievingly, although he had known for some time that the end was near. He stayed staring, oblivious of the child standing beside him, a thumb in her mouth. Then she clutched his sleeve, saying nothing.

He bent down and put his arm round her. Her little body was rigid with fear. He picked her up gently, moved to a chair and sat her on his knee. How could he explain death to a young child, he wondered?"

"Meg, you remember the bird that died last month?"

Meg solemnly nodded.

"Well, your mother has died. Just like the bird."

Meg considered.

"Shall we have to bury her in the garden?"

"Yes, but not in the garden. In the cemetery."

A pause.

"Then we shan't see her again?"

"No."

Child and father together shared the awesome implications of this statement.

Tears welled up in the little girl's eyes.

"Father?"

"Yes?"

"You won't die too will you?"

"Everybody in the world will die one day," he said gently. "But no, I'm not going to leave you. Now come with me to find Mary because I have to tell George and make a lot of arrangements."

Meg scrambled down obediently tightly holding his hand. From now on he would have to be father and mother to the child.

136

"Say goodbye to your mother," said William. But she turned her head away and covered her face. Still shaken, he led her out of the room.

(3)

A large gathering assembled at the kirk for Margaret Hay's funeral. It was a fine day with a chilly breeze and the waves in the harbour were edged with white. Clouds flecked with ochre and grey hung over the low green hills around the little town, gulls screeched and drifted down the air currents and then soared back up again over the houses.

Six men carried the coffin, and a lone fiddler played a plaintive tune as it headed the procession, followed by William and his children in mourning, and other relations. The Church of Scotland was built on land that William himself had donated in the years of his prosperity. After the service Margaret was laid to rest in the little graveyard to the south of the town, overlooking Bressay Sound, the newly-chiselled gravestone looking doubly white against the background of blue sky, blue sea and green hills.

As William and his family stood near the grave to receive condolences his brother Andrew clasped him by the arm. No words were necessary to share their emotion. Others followed and then suddenly William was taken aback to see Martha Ogilvy coming towards him, holding out her hand.

"I had to come," she said simply. "Life's too short to bear a grudge."

Almost speechless, William seized her outstretched fingers in their black gloves. His eyes moistened with tears.

"Thank you," he murmured in a low voice.

She smiled. "Come and see us at Seafield," she said.

He nodded.

And then she was gone, and there were other relations and friends to greet.

When he had time to consider the matter, in spite of his grief over his wife's death, William was aware that a heavy weight had been lifted from his soul.

(4)

Soon after the funeral William went south to Edinburgh again. He had legal business and financial affairs to attend to and did not intend to be there long. He stayed with his daughter Barbara and her husband Henry Cheyne and their children, and met a number of friends and family while he was there.

One night at a concert as he was being introduced to several acquaintances, Henry said, "This is Mr MacPherson and his wife. Mr William Hay. I think you both know Aberdeen well."

The man was large, in black with white hair and side-whiskers. His wife was also white-haired, tall and plump and she wore a deep blue dress and a black wrap.

"Why William!" said the woman, suddenly recognising him as he continued to smile and hold out his hand. "Don't you remember me? Edward, William used to come and visit our home in Aberdeen when I was young. I was Eleanor Maclean."

William cast his mind back to his student days and seemed to be trying to reconcile this worn but smiling woman with the handsome young girl he had known. Either his memory was playing him false or she had changed beyond recognition. This wasn't the first time he had met old schoolfriends or acquaintances he hadn't seen for years, but sometimes they hardly seemed to have altered at all. Eleanor's glorious head of golden hair, her youthful smile, her graceful figure and her light step, all had gone. At first he felt angered that time should have changed her so much. Then he realised with a shock that he had probably altered too. He had to admit that he wouldn't have recognised her if she hadn't spoken. Then gradually as they talked he began to remember some of her mannerisms and realised she was still as intelligent, kind and outgoing as ever. He tried hard to recall those emotions he had felt when still a callow youth, for she had been his first love though he had never told her how he felt. It was all such a long time ago. He had met many people, and married and buried two wives since then.

"You had to leave Aberdeen in a hurry," Eleanor was saying. "We were good friends. It was sad we never met again."

She went on to tell him they spent most of the year in Edinburgh, and that her husband was a successful and respected lawyer. She had had ten children, eight of them still alive.

"I'm sorry to hear of the death of your wife," she added, as he explained. "Edward, William Hay must come and visit us before he leaves."

When they parted, William thought to himself how precious and fragile first love was. All those powerful emotions, all that heartbreak, ended up like this.

Then Eleanor vanished from his thoughts and only the pale suffering face of his recently deceased wife remained with him. Time, he supposed, would even steal her memory away.

(5)

When he returned to Lerwick William buried himself in his work. Earlier that year George had come into the counting-house one day with the news that a ship from Aberdeen was in port and was bound to the Davis Straits to fish for cod. William always kept a careful note of all the shipping in the harbour, and their business, because although the steamer *Sovereign* now made a regular run each week from Aberdeen with the mail as well as passengers, it was still often useful to send letters by the first available ship. Besides, he liked to keep abreast of new developments, and the idea of crews going off beyond Greenland, where the whalers went, to fish for cod, was an exciting new venture. About the time his wife had been due back from Madeira he had decided to send off the *Janet Hay* to the same destination. Fishing off Faroe had proved useful, but new fishing grounds were also needed. In characteristic fashion he dreamed of having a whole fleet of schooners, and signing up Shetlanders still out of work, many of whom were deciding to emigrate in the hopes of a better future. But although he did soon have other ships, William was not in a financial position to carry out his ideas. Nor was the first season very successful.

Nevertheless the firm was beginning to pay its way, and William gradually realised to his relief that he was once more being accepted and respected by other merchants in the district. This may have been partly due to the fact that he was now appointed vice-consul for Denmark, the post Charles Ogilvy had held. It meant that he was responsible for the welfare of any Danish seamen who called in to Shetland, whether from Denmark, Iceland or Faroe, especially any that were shipwrecked and stranded without the means to get home. He had to see that any sick Danish sailor received medical attention. He also had to give hospitality to any Danish visitors who came to Lerwick.

William also sent out a consignment of fish to Calcutta, where his son William, who had left the bank in Edinburgh, had now gone to work as a merchant. He was constantly exploring new outlets, always looking for new ideas. His many and varied duties left him little time to himself, but he was satisfied with his work and began to revel in hopes of success.

CHAPTER THIRTEEN
Another Dream Realised

William was not the only person to suffer tragedy during 1846. A blight caused the potatoes to rot, and as the local people relied on potatoes and fish as their staple foods, they soon found themselves with very little to eat. The failure of the potato crop had started in Ireland, where it caused widespread famine, and spread to Scotland and then to Shetland. In the face of untold distress the authorities in Shetland applied to the government asking for money to build roads and give employment to the destitute. At first they refused, but then they did agree to arrange for the distribution of meal through sixteen local distress committees in return for work. Local charitable women set up a soup kitchen in Lerwick to feed the hungry, and William Hay bought in rice and maize in an attempt to alleviate the situation. But the relief operations had been somewhat haphazardly organised and the local community had been unable to prevent all the population from wanting to share in the relief, such were the close ties and feelings of solidarity among the inhabitants. A few isolated stretches of road were built, but the experiment was not a success.

At the end of 1847 the government appointed Captain Craigie to be Resident Inspector of Relief in Shetland. William Hay met him when he arrived and entertained him at Hayfield. Captain Craigie had been in the Navy and served in the Mediterranean and also taken part in many anti-slavery patrols. Now he was retired on half pay and received this new appointment gratefully. He was given a house on the outskirts of Lerwick and paid travelling expenses to cover his journeys for the Central Board of Relief.

William found they shared a number of views in common and discussed the worsening situation with him. Then Captain Craigie left for a tour of the islands, which took him three months. When William heard that he was back he issued an early invitation as he was anxious to discover his findings and learn what he proposed to do. William himself was in despair at the number of desperate people who applied to him for help and could see no way out.

"It's a grim situation," began Captain Craigie, as they sat drinking together after a meal. "It's not helped by the system of tenancy that seems to operate here in Shetland. The way the people hold their crofts in return for their fishing makes them too dependent on their landlords, and when they do have a little money they are reluctant to spend it on their crofts in case their landlord raises the rent. Result, persistent poverty."

"The danger is that they become dependent on handouts," said William, "and do nothing to help themselves. But I don't see any other solution."

"Well, it may sound harsh," said Captain Craigie," but instead of doing a little work in return for meal, I think they should be made to work full-time. And the relief should be a mere subsistence so that they will only accept it in a real emergency. Only one member of a family should get relief – you've no idea what cheating has been going on in some places."

"You don't understand how the people think up here," said William smiling. "They wouldn't call it cheating."

"Well, I'm proposing to distribute meal early this year, before the people are forced to eat their seed. From what I've seen of your tough Shetland fishermen, they will find it less demanding and less dangerous building roads than going to sea. And we've got to find some way to ensuring that those who go off on the whalers to Greenland, pay their wives while they are away."

"We always hold back part of their pay for their wives and families," said William.

"Yes, but can you be sure they receive it?" asked Captain Craigie. "A lot of them seem to stay in Lerwick and go on a spending spree when they return. I've been thinking a lot while I've been away. I think the initial proposal to make men build roads for relief was a sound one. Firstly Shetland badly needs roads, and it would give the sailors an incentive to go straight home when they get back to Lerwick if they could get there easily by road. It would also allow Lerwick to expand as a market for goods."

"I entirely agree with you, said William. "It was always one of my dreams for the future to help provide roads in Shetland."

"Well, that's what I'm suggesting," said Captain Craigie, pleased to find he had at least one landowner agreeing with him. "I'm suggesting that the workers be paid in cash wages, and the local proprietors should contribute up to one third of the cost. They will take responsibility for those parts of the roads that pass through their estates, and they will obviously benefit more than anybody from a proper road system. Do you think most of them will agree?"

William said he couldn't say. Compared to the mainland, Shetland was a rather backward place, and some of the lairds refused to move with the times.

"Not only backward," said Captain Craigie. "When I was up in Yell a Norwegian ship bound for Venice was wrecked on the coast during a heavy gale. The crew fortunately got ashore and found their way to the schoolmaster's house. He set twenty men to guard the wreck but they refused to stay all night and by next morning anything of value had been taken away. Apparently hundreds of people just came down to the beach and helped themselves to anything they could find, in the most open manner. They had even got on board the wreck and were breaking up the ship with hatchets to see what they could find. And what I find even more shameful is that the laird who is also the local magistrate, refused to see the harm in it!"

William sighed.

"The local people see things differently," he said. "They see a wreck as an act of God and an opportunity for them to harvest the fruits of the sea. I've come up against this too. There have been eight wrecks round our coasts this year. Recently Hay and Son have been engaged in trying to help salvage some of the cargoes for the owners, and I can see things from your point of view. But not everyone understands it."

"Well, on the whole they are grand folk," conceded Captain Craigie. "Very hospitable even when they have so little. Very independent-minded though," he added. "No time for the authorities. I shall go home and start to put all this in motion. I shall be in touch soon."

(2)

The first road constructed was from Lerwick to Scalloway but it was poorly built and was little better than a footpath. Over the next years real progress was made. William was required to assist in the building of the road from Lerwick to Dunrossness, together with other landowners including John Bruce of Sumburgh and the Earl of Zetland. Over his stretch of road William employed twenty-two men and three boys. It was difficult work, cutting through rocks and building retaining walls of dry stone three feet high. In other places the ground was soft bog and needed many yards of earth embankments.

William took an active interest in the road-building programme, and often went to see what progress was being made. One mild spring day on the hilly stretch of road above Sandlodge, with the island of Mousa in the distance, he reined in his horse and looked about him.

Over eighty people were hard at work road building. One group were shoring up the side of the road, another deepening the ditches, while most of them were working with picks to level the road surface. While they loosened the rocks, women and boys removed the pieces and spread out the loose stones and earth to form the roadway.

As William approached they looked up cheerfully and he felt that although it was hard labour they were working with a will. When the foreman walked over to talk to William he signalled to the men with picks to take a few minutes' rest.

"This is a difficult stretch," he said, excusing his lenience. "They're not making as much progress as before. But they consider themselves lucky to have been taken on. At least it means food for their families."

William stopped for some time inspecting the different tasks and talking to one or two people, one of them a poor woman he had helped to get the job. As he gazed idly at the workmen he found a dark-haired, rather wild-eyed man eyeing him with a strange look. Something stirred in his memory.

"Ask that man to come here," he said to the foreman.

The man, realising he had been singled out, approached hesitatingly. But there was a look of repressed resentment in his eyes.

"Were you working for Hay and Ogilvy's?" asked William not unkindly.

"No sir. I didn't work at Freefield. I come from Laxfirth."

Suddenly William remembered where he had seen his face before. The picture of an old woman lying on the ground in a miserable hovel, refusing to leave her home, came back into his mind. And this was the young man who had been with her when they had been evicted. What had happened to them since? He was on the point of asking. Then, "I took you for someone else," he said brusquely.

But the man had recognised him too.

He bowed his head and moved away. William reined in his horse and turned its head. As he rode off a momentary feeling of regret filled him for circumstances it was too late to change. Then he thought how strange it was that his dream of building roads should have at last been realised, even if he had had to wait for a natural disaster to overtake the island for it to come true.

CHAPTER FOURTEEN

Calm Waters

In the autumn of his life, fortune began to favour William again. He had the assistance of an able clerk, and his son George continued to support him. The firm cured fish all over Shetland, even in the North Isles, owned a whole fleet of ships, and set up stores in a number of different places. William bought back Freefield and Blacksness at Scalloway, and with the help of his brother Andrew, regained yet more property in Lerwick, the Tingwall Valley and Whiteness. But to his sorrow he was never able to return to Laxfirth, where he had memories of his father and where he had lavished much time and energy on improvements.

His later years were saddened by the loss of family and friends. Jeremiah Malcomson, the likeable young man who had set up the store in Scalloway, left the harbour one day in a small boat with a fellow oarsman, to deliver a cargo of salt to the fishing station on the island of Burra. It was the middle of August and the weather clear, but as quite often happened, the sky suddenly grew black, and the wind freshened. The boat was later found abandoned with oars, sail and cargo intact. Two bodies were discovered on the shore. William was very moved when the news was brought to him of the disaster.

Several years later in 1852 the mailboat *William Hogarth* was lost with all hands in a storm. The tragedy shocked the local population and a good merchant friend of William's was among those drowned. William was also grieved to learn of the deaths of two of the captains of his ships who over the years had also become good friends. One was lost overboard in rough weather near Sumburgh Head; the other died of smallpox on the way up the west coast of Scotland and was buried in a small churchyard there. William paid to have an inscription put there by the firm.

In 1854 came the news from New York that his younger brother James had also died. William had not seen him since he had set out for New Brunswick all those years ago, but they had kept in touch by letter and his death came as a personal blow. A whole era had passed away and times were changing.

(2)

In 1855 William went down south to Edinburgh to visit family and friends. He took the train from Aberdeen, which made the journey a lot quicker. During his stay he received many invitations to dine out. He always enjoyed company but on this occasion found himself sitting at the opposite end of the table to a very striking-looking woman. She wasn't young, and she wasn't pretty, but her face with a pale almost white complexion and a head of short dark hair, was intelligent and almost beautiful. As he looked in her direction he caught her eye, and her eyes were dark and honest. She blushed slightly as he continued to stare almost rudely and looked modestly away. But when she looked again towards him, she saw he hadn't taken his eyes off her.

"Can you tell me the name of the woman at the end of the table?" he asked his opposite partner earnestly.

The man glanced down the table and said," That's Isabella Sanderson. Her father's a minister from Inverkeithing."

"Is she married?"

"She's a widow."

"Can you tell me more about her?"

The man looked at William amused.

"Would you like me to introduce you to her?" he asked.

When the meal was over and the evening entertainment began, William found himself sitting on a sofa next to Isabella in earnest conversation. They had begun as total strangers, but within a short space of time they had found a topic that interested them both, and became quite engrossed. Some spark of attraction had passed between them. William felt it himself, and was almost sure that she felt the same way.

Before the evening was out William realised that he had fallen in love. At sixty-eight he was experiencing feelings he hadn't known for years. He had met many women and found some attractive, but this was more akin to the emotions he had felt all those years ago for Eleanor Maclean. He was fit and active and his years of success and sorrow had given him a distinguished look. He had been a widower for nine years now and until this moment had had no intention of marrying again. Now he knew for sure that what he most wanted in life was to marry this woman. He was determined not to let her go without making arrangements to see her again.

They agreed to meet each other in two day's time, and spent another happy evening enjoying each other's company. From then on they somehow managed to meet every day, to drink coffee, eat ices, or drive out in a chaise together down fashionable Princes Street. Eventually when he summoned up the courage to tell her how he felt, he discovered that she had felt the same way about him, from the very first moment. Up till then, she confessed, she had firmly decided to remain unattached. Then this elderly Shetlander, much older than she was, twice a widower and father of numerous children, had suddenly swept her off her feet with an aplomb she could not resist.

William's head was in a whirl. It had all happened so suddenly. They planned to marry by special licence as soon as possible. He rejoiced that Hayfield would soon have a new mistress and that he would have the pleasure of introducing her to his family and friends. They would be as surprised as he was.

Suddenly his life seemed to have moved into calmer waters once again. He had found, quite unexpectedly, a new partner and a new source of joy. He reflected that happiness was possible at any stage in life and it always stole upon you unawares.

(3)

Three happy years went by. Isabella was a woman of strong character and immense personal resources, who managed in a short while to turn Hayfield into a home once again. She captured the heart of little Meg, tamed young Arthur, and even got on good terms with George, who might so easily have resented her new intimacy with his father. Mary and Thomas returned from school in Montrose and Aberdeen to a stable atmosphere and a sense of security. Above all, she gave William the love and support he craved.

Nearly every day he went to his counting-house and continued to take an interest in all that went on. Isabella, whose intelligence was not satisfied with running the household, listened patiently to his talk of business, in a way neither Margaret Ogilvy nor Margaret Scott had been able to do.

William was fond of reminiscing about his childhood and youth, those seemingly carefree days before he went south to Scotland, when there were no roads in Shetland, and when people travelled long distances by open boat. He recalled the days of the press-gangs and of the soldiers and naval officers who came up to Lerwick during the war, and used to visit his father. He talked of his schooldays in Aberdeen, and how Aberdeen used to be, and he mentioned with nostalgia his time as a student at King's, a year when he had tasted freedom and dreamed dreams. He and Isabella would sit companionably near a warm peat fire of a winter's evening and she enjoyed listening to his memories which brought the past alive to her.

He told her how, because of his father's illness, he had had to come home, and help with the business.

"It's strange how life works out," he reflected, as the flames flickered and lit up their faces. "I never wanted to become a merchant."

"I find that difficult to believe," said Isabella.

"Perhaps when we're young we don't know what's good for us," said William thoughtfully. "Circumstances mould us more than we think. Now George has always wanted to follow in my footsteps. And Andrew seemed to have it in his blood. But I thought I wanted something different."

"Perhaps it was always in your character to see a bit further than the others," said Isabella softly. "You are different. I knew it as soon as I met you. That's why I wanted to marry you. That's why I love you."

Tears came into his eyes as she laid her hand gently on his arm.

(4)

One fine summer's day William sat at his polished wooden desk alone in the counting-house writing a letter. Down one wall the shelves were filled with thick leather-bound books, ledgers, daybooks, and boxes of letters. The room was panelled in light oak and by the window were two tables with other chairs with leather seats and tall backs, edged with gleaming brass studs. Inkwells, quill pens, sheets of paper and piles of correspondence waiting to be answered lay on the tables. On the mantelpiece stood a large plain clock ticking steadily away. Through the window could be seen boats tied up in the harbour and gulls swooping over the water.

William paused and suddenly saw himself in his father's counting-house as a boy with its bare walls and small high window. It was all so long ago, yet it seemed but yesterday. How different things were now! And what had he achieved? At one time he would probably have claimed to have achieved much, but since his bankruptcy his perspectives had changed. He had done his best, that was all. Life had been good to him in the end; his hard work had been rewarded with several years of happiness and peace of mind. The firm was flourishing. His daughter Meg, now nearly thirteen, was at school in Aberdeen and growing up fast. All the others had left home. George was now married and had a son. William saw his brother Andrew nearly every week. And he had the love and companionship of his new wife Isabella. Could one ask for more?

He smiled to himself. Many scenes from his childhood flashed through his mind as vividly as if they had been yesterday. His father, Aunt Grace, his schooldays in Aberdeen, his apprenticeship in Hull, his eldest son James. The present scene, with the sunlight lighting up the room, seemed very distant. He suddenly felt very weary.

When several minutes later George came into the counting-house it was very quiet. His father was lying across his desk and his pen had dropped from his hand. George laid a hand on his father's shoulder and realised he was not breathing. He stood there a moment stunned. He glanced at the letter his father had been writing.

"Dear Sir," it began," Regarding the consignment of herring we promised you...."

Admiration mingled with dismay and grief in George's mind. William had been faithful to the very end. And now it was up to him to carry on the business.

He went rapidly to the door and out into the warehouse.

"Come quickly," he called urgently. "I need your help. Mr Hay is dead."

(5)

He was buried in the little graveyard overlooking Bressay Sound, next to his two wives. Letters of condolence reached Isabella from far and wide, praising his good qualities, his perseverance, courage and enterprise. The one she treasured most did not come from a close relative or friend but from a fellow merchant in Aberdeen. "In spite of all his personal tragedies, and the disaster which hit him when Hay and Ogilvy's collapsed," he wrote, "he was always honest and trustworthy in business, dependable as a merchant, and an example to us all."